THE LAST PIRATE HANGED

THE TRUE ADVENTURES OF CAPTAIN WILLIAM SWALLOW

&

THE SHIP WITH NO NAME

G. S WILLMOTT

BOOKS BY G S WILLMOTT

The Other Side of the Trench – The Spirit of War
Brothers in Arms
Escape
Red Lights on the Somme
Survival
Soul Survivor
You Forgot the Sauce – An Alzheimer's Journey You Won't Forget
Boy's Own War
Serendipity – A Gallipoli Love Story
Colour Blind – Bullets and Shell Don't Discriminate
Global Warming – A Weapon of Mass Destruction
Small Farm Warriors
1000-Yard Stare

Children's
The Importance of Being Ivy

FUTURE RELEASES
Gangsters & Whores'
The Fab Sixties

Children's
The Importance of Being Truthful

CONTENTS

LONDON A CITY OF SQUALOR

CHAPTER 1

White Chapel London 1825

In the Edwardian era, London had become the fastest growing city in the world. With such growth came squalor, sewage in the streets, both animal and human in origin, the ubiquitous rats scurrying about and the children in the rags they called clothes playing soccer or getting up to mischief.

It was difficult for the poorer classes to make enough to feed their families, but some could earn a penny or two acting as porters. Young boys could earn a halfpenny tending a horse while the driver took a break. Others would sell newspapers or sell snacks their mothers and sisters had prepared.

The filthy Thames would quite often surrender something of value to the mudlarks who would then on-sell it to vendors in the street.

The beggars were prolific; often working with young children who had been blinded.

The prostitutes were as common as the rats and street urchins; all in all Whitechapel was not a desirable place to live.

Dorset Street Whitechapel

This was the environment where William Swallow, aka Walker, aka Brown was raised. At fourteen, he joined His Majesty's Navy in order to escape from the filth and degradation.

Life at sea was hard; he experienced several floggings for insubordination, but he didn't have a moment of regret. He got to see the world and became an experienced mariner.

Swallow's first voyage to Canton, China, was in 1826 aboard the ship *Prince of Wales*, a 120-gun man of war. The ship's assignment was to escort several British merchant ships from the East India Company who intended to trade with the Chinese.

The merchants traded British woollens and Indian cotton for Chinese tea, porcelain and silk. The popularity of tea in England ensured this commodity became the single largest trading item between the two nations. It didn't take long for a significant trade imbalance to occur in China's favour.

Silver became the precious metal China sought, but a shortage of the commodity made it difficult for the British to pay for the tea.

The British realised they needed another commodity to trade and they discovered opium, a highly lucrative substance.

Although never directly involved in the sale of opium, which was banned in China by an Imperial edict in1729 as an illegal drug, the East India Company was responsible for most of its production in India, mainly for its medicinal value. The actual business of selling opium was conducted through private agencies.

Young William, being way down the pecking order, was also near last in rations received. He decided he needed to supplement his meagre diet with some nutritious food. He became proficient in stealing from the officer's larder. Unfortunately, he was caught and thrown in the brig where he stayed for the entire return voyage.

William married his childhood sweetheart Susan during his first shore leave in 1827.

His son John was conceived during William's second shore leave.

When the *Prince of Wales* docked at Portsmouth he was summarily court-marshalled and expelled from the service.

William had nowhere to go but back to Whitechapel. He moved back into a room in Whitechapel Road with his family and cogitated over his future. He decided he would join the Merchant Navy.

In the meantime he needed to feed his wife and family as well as paying the rent. There was only one solution; break into a house and steal goods that were easily disposed of.

He selected Knightsbridge and chose the house of Lord Denman, the Lord Chief Justice of England. Not that Swallow knew who the master of this grand house was at the time…

Lord Denman

Young William waited until midnight before breaking into the manor house via a window unlocked at the back of the residence. He slid through and with the aid of a candle began searching for appropriate plunder. He spotted a pair of silver candelabra and slid them into his canvas bag. He returned to the open window and had begun his exit when he felt a tug on his left leg.

'Where do you think you're going, young man?' asked the head butler. His name was George Turner.

'Oh, nowhere. I was just—'

'You were just stealing my master's best silver.'

'I'm sorry. Here, take them and I'll be on my way.'

'I will take them but you won't be on your way, lad. I'm taking you down to the police station. They can decide what to do with you.'

Mr Turner locked William in the cellar with the help of a Purdy shotgun. In the morning he escorted the frightened young man to the local police station where he was locked in a cell awaiting trial.

William knew he would either be sentenced to hang or, if he was lucky, he might be transported to Australia. The other issue he had was that at twenty-eight, he had a wife and two children who he loved very much. Either way, William knew he wouldn't see his wife and children again.

White Chapel Magistrates Court 1827

The magistrate on duty was Harold Lloyd. He was known for his propensity to hand out the death sentence.

The clerk of the court called out William's name and he was required to stand in the dock.

The crimes were read out. They comprised breaking and entering and stealing.

'I believe the prisoner was caught red-handed in the house of Lord Denman.'

'Yes that is correct, Your Honour.' replied the clerk.

'I also believe the prisoner is married with two young children?'

'That's correct, Your Honour.'

'Well, you should have thought of the effect your actions would have on your family, Swallow.

'I hereby sentence you, William Swallow, to transportation for the term of your natural life. Take him down.'

Swallow, now a convicted felon, was manhandled down the stairs and placed in a cell along with ten other recently convicted men.

After a very cold and uncomfortable night, all eleven prisoners were bundled into a horse-drawn covered wagon. They all assumed they were heading for the docks to board a ship bound for Botany Bay.

They were heading for the docks all, right but not to sail to Australia, or at least not yet. Their destination was the *Discovery*, one of the ships in Captain Cook's fleet during his famous voyage of discovery. It was now relegated to be a prison hulk anchored on the Thames.

The Discovery

The prisoners were transferred to a longboat. All were in chains, which would remain on their wrists and ankles for the duration of their stay on the rotting hulk.

Once William and his fellow prisoners arrived at the *Discovery* they were required to climb a rope ladder and clamber onto the deck.

The Superintendent in charge of the hulk was Mr Francis Armitage, a seasoned officer of the prison system. He had worked at Newgate Prison for most of his adult life.

He addressed the motley group prior to them being taken down to their new home.

'My name is Mr Armitage. I am ultimately responsible for your wellbeing while you are imprisoned on this hulk. When I say wellbeing, I mean if you behave yourselves and follow my officers' orders you won't be flogged within an inch of your lives. We have a cat on board, the cat of nine tails. Try and keep away from her.

'Take them down Mr Bridges.'

Although the prison quarters were spartan, the prisoners were not locked in cells and after dark they were free to wander around the deck.

On the first morning of William's incarceration, he was woken at 5 am and ordered to roll up his hammock. The ward was unlocked and the prisoners were able to wash and dress in a uniform ready for the new day…

and what a day it would be! Next was breakfast, consisting of twelve ounces of bread and one pint of cocoa.

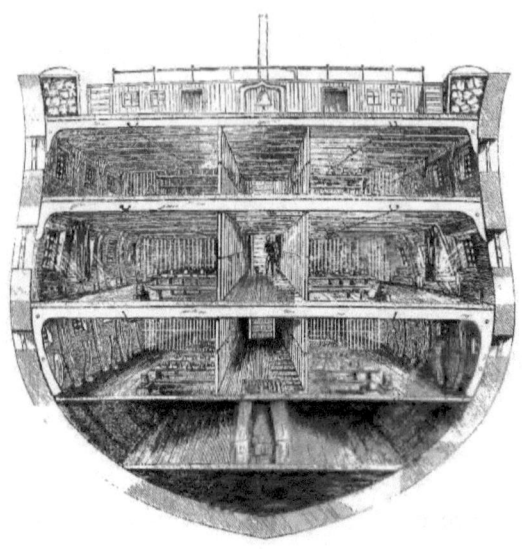

SECTIONAL VIEW OF THE INTERIOR OF THE "DEFENCE" HULK.

William commented to the prisoner next to him.

'This isn't too bad, is it?'

Immediately, William felt a sharp pain in the back of his head.

'Shut up. No talking at breakfast. Do it again and I'll belt you even harder,' said the guard.

Swallow never uttered a sound at breakfast again.

WASHING-ROOM.

Once the dry bread and cocoa were consumed by all the prisoners, they were required to thoroughly clean all the decks until 7.30 am.

Having completed the cleaning, all the men were mustered in gangs and rowed out to work on the docks. Officers and guards were waiting to supervise the convicts to unload timber and ballast from the ships. Other tasks included dredging channels and clearing rubble.

William, being a newly convicted prisoner, found it difficult to carry the timber while being locked in chains. He fell over three times and each time he was whipped by one of the guards.

When lunchtime arrived all the prisoners were rowed back to the hulk to eat their lunch and after an hour they were rowed back to the dock to continue their hard labour.

Conversations between convicts and free labourers were permitted on the basis of the dangerous work being undertaken.

William was carrying a heavy beam with the assistance of a free worker. They reached their destination and placed the heavy oak beam on the far side of the dock.

As they returned for the next beam, William asked the worker where he lived. He thought it was a simple question, but the guard who heard the conversation didn't think so.

'Hey, you come here. You're not allowed to converse with the freemen unless it related to your work. Come with me I'll teach you a lesson.'

With the help of another guard, he grabbed William and tied him to the whipping triangle.

'I'm giving you thirty lashes; a very light sentence, considering.'

On the thirtieth stroke, they untied William and instructed him to return to work with blood soaking his shirt.

The lesson was learned. William never spoke to a free worker again other than about work-related issues.

The convicts would count down the clock waiting for 5 o'clock.

The men were then rowed back to the hulk where they would wash before supper. Their meal comprised of six ounces of meat, invariably as tough as an old boot. To accompany the meat was one pound of potatoes and nine ounces of bread. It was the same menu every night.

After the evening meal the convicts were expected to attend evening prayers.

Then they had schoolwork. Many of the men were illiterate when they arrived on the hulk and literate when they departed.

Mathew was already literate so these lessons were irrelevant to him. One of the prisoners had been a navigator in a previous life and he offered to teach the young mariner the skill of navigation.

Mathew took to his lessons like a fish to water and after a year, he was capable of navigating the seven seas.

The young convict enjoyed the evenings when the men could wander around the deck conversing with other prisoners and enjoying the odd pipe and totty of rum which had been smuggled onto the hulk.

THE DECK OF THE "DEFENCE" HOSPITAL SHIP.

BOUND FOR BOTANY BAY

CHAPTER 2

March 3, 1828

Mathew and several other prisoners from the *Discovery* were notified that they would be transferred to the HMS *Exmouth* for transportation to New South Wales.

The *Exmouth* had been moored close to the *Discovery* in the Thames; enabling easy transfer to the vessel.

There were 40 convicts in the longboat ready to join the other 250 convicts for the five-month journey of hell to the colony of New South Wales.

Once aboard the prisoners were read the ship's rules. Those who broke them would be severely punished.

The master of the ship addressed his human cargo.

He enunciated the ship's rules, some of which were:

1. The prisoners must conduct themselves in a respectful and becoming manner to all the officers on board and they are strictly to obey such orders as I may issue through the Captain of Divisions and Heads of Messes.
2. The prisoners must behave themselves in a decent and becoming manner at all times but more especially when prayers are had at Divine Service, performed prayers morning and evening, weather permitting.
3. Cursing and all foul language, shouting, quarrelling, fighting, selling, exchanging or giving away clothes are strictly forbidden.
4. Any person stealing or secreting any of the ship's stores or any other article belonging to the stores in the ship will be severely punished.
5. The prisoners are on no occasion to hold conversation with the guard or Ship's Company or talk through bars below.
6. Each mess shall have a captain and it will be the duty of each man in his turn to clean the utensils, the latter after each meal are to be

taken on deck and thoroughly cleansed before being passed below, and the members of each mess are to sit together.

7. The captains of messes are warned that they will be held responsible for the good order and cleanliness of the mess; they are to see that the men wash themselves every morning and that they attend to them and ensure there are no men sleeping with their clothes on.

8. Smoking or striking lights below in the prison, washing or attempting to dry clothes will not be allowed under any pretence whatever.

William soon made friends among the prisoners on his deck. Two in particular, George Davis and William Watts, became close mates. These men were in hammocks either side of William.

The routine on the ship remained the same each day for the five months of the journey.

4.00 a.m. Prisoner cooks (3 in number) admitted on deck.

5.30 a.m. Captains of divisions and upper deck for the purpose of filling wash tubs and prisoners at the same time to commence taking up their beds and hammocks.

6.00 a.m. One half of the prisoners admitted for the purpose of washing their person under the supervision of their respective captains half an hour being allowed for this purpose.

7.30 a.m. Down all prisoners. Ships company to commence washing upper deck and water closets.

8.00 a.m. Breakfast.

8.30 a.m. One man from each mess admitted on deck for the purpose of washing up their mess utensils.

9.00 a.m. All the prisoners admitted on deck with the exception of the men in each mess who in turn will clean and scrape dry the prison deck and their berths the bottom boards of the latter being removed during which time I will attend in the surgery and on the deck.

9.30 a.m. Prison inspected after which all the prisoners will be assembled on deck for prayers.

10.00 a.m. One half of the prisoners sent on deck for exercise the other half being arranged in schools under the superintendence of the Religious Instructor assisted by monitors.

11.30 a.m. School to break up.

12.00 a.m. Dinner.

12.30 p.m. From each mess one man to be admitted on deck for the purpose of washing mess utensils.

1.20 p.m. Deck to be swept up.

1.30 p.m. Half the prisoners to be admitted on deck the remainder below to be arranged in school as in the forenoon.

4.00 p.m. Down all beds and hammocks.

4.30 p.m. Supper.

5.00 p.m. One man from each mess admitted on deck to wash utensils.

6.30 p.m. Prayers.

7.00 p.m. Petty officers of the day and night muster on deck.

8.00 p.m. Down all prisoners.

9.00 p.m. Rounds.

Apart from very rough seas when passing the Cape of Good Hope the voyage was uneventful and no prisoners died en route.

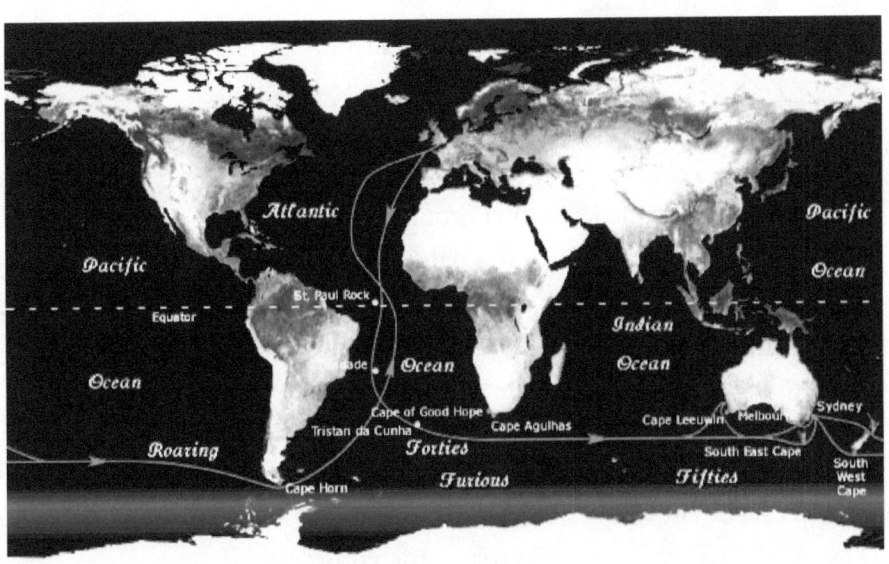

Mathew Swallow and the other 294 prisoners were below deck, as usual, and the ship was heaving in the turbulent ocean. Many of the prisoners were suffering from seasickness. The buckets they were using were being thrown around the deck, spilling the vomit over the floor, making it impossible to navigate. These horrendous conditions prevailed for five days. Normal mealtimes were cancelled and bread and water were the only provisions available to the men.

'I don't know how much more of this I can take, mate.'

'You'll be right, Willy. It can't go on forever.'

'It already feels like for fucking forever. My guts is so fucking sore from heaving.'

'Just try and drink some water. That'll help.

'What water? It's been spilled all over the deck.'

'I'll see if I can get some more from down the other end.'

Mathew grabbed a bucket and walked to the far end of the deck.

'Can you blokes spare some water? All ours went over.'

'Fuck off. We need it all.'

'I'm not asking for much— half a bucket would be enough.'

'I said, fuck off.'

Undeterred, Mathew crossed over to the other side of the deck, slipping and sliding as he went.

He was able to persuade another group to spare him half a bucket.

He thanked them and began the dangerous return journey back to Willy. He nearly fell over several times but he made it back with most of the precious cargo intact.

'Here you go, mate. Drink this cup of water. It'll settle your guts.'

The next morning the *Exmouth* sailed into calmer waters. The prisoners were ordered to clean the decks thoroughly; not a very pleasant task with vomit and excrement all over the decks.

The ship's master, Daniel Warren, ordered groups of forty under chains up onto the main deck to breathe the fresh sea air. This procession continued all day until the entire prison population had experienced the joy of clean air in their lungs.

The calm weather morphed into the doldrums and the *Exmouth* was becalmed.

'I don't understand what's happening, Captain Warren. We should be sailing at full speed. We passed 40 degrees latitude yesterday. What's happened to the Roaring Forties?'

'I'm just as confused as you, Lieutenant. I've sailed this route three times before. The Roaring Forties hit us just after we rounded the Cape of Good Hope every time.'

'Maybe we need to be patient and pray to God for fair winds.'

'That's about the only thing we can do,' said Captain Warren.

Captain Warren decided to retire for the night. After he entered his cabin, he poured a brandy and contemplated his predicament. He was paid a bonus if he could make port by July 30, but if the forties didn't arrive soon and fill the *Exmouth*'s sails he would arrive late.

He hoped things would be different by morning.

When Captain Warren rose at 6 am, he got out of bed and was thrown to the far side of the cabin. He pulled himself up from the cabin floor and was thrown back to where he started.

What in God's name is happening to my ship? he thought.

He managed to dress, not worrying about washing and clambered up the stairs up to the main deck.

The sea's huge waves were breaking over the bow and the deck was awash. He saw Lieutenant Worthington holding on to the mainsail rope.

'Lieutenant, I think our prayers have been answered. The Roaring Forties have arrived.'

'I think they have, Captain. I was waiting for you to be on deck before I ordered all the sails to be lowered.'

'Lower the sails? Certainly not! We need to make up time.'

The adrenaline was pumping through the Captain's veins and he was willing the *Exmouth* to go even faster.

From his position, he could observe the helmsman at the end of the deck battling to hold course. The *Exmouth* wasn't under full sail, but the sails set were almost bursting.

The experienced mariner seemed to be enthralled by the sounds of his ship being pushed to the absolute limit. The cacophony of the seas and wind ripping through the sails excited him.

Captain Warren may have been enjoying the experience but the cargo below was not.

The prisoners were being thrown about with very little to grab onto. Several prisoners had suffered broken arms and legs, but the ship's surgeon was nowhere to be seen. He had no intention of leaving his cabin.

William had suffered significant bruising of his ribs albeit no breaks, but he suffered acute seasickness once again and hoped he would die.

These conditions lasted for twenty-four hours and then settled down. The Roaring Forties continued to provide the wind but not at gale force; they would ensure the *Exmouth* would arrive in Port Jackson on time.

I NOW CALL AUSTRALIA HOME

CHAPTER 3

July 28, 1828

The *Exmouth* sailed into Port Jackson in the early afternoon. The seas were calm and the winds were favourable. The ship's company were all on deck admiring the harbour and the shoreline. The prisoners had no such view; that morning they had their chains fitted ready for disembarking in what most of them would call their home for the rest of their lives.

A muster was held on board by the Colonial Secretary. The information included name, age, education, religion, marital status, family, native place, trade, offence, when and where tried, sentence, previous convictions, physical description and who the prisoners were assigned to on arrival.

Port Jackson 1828

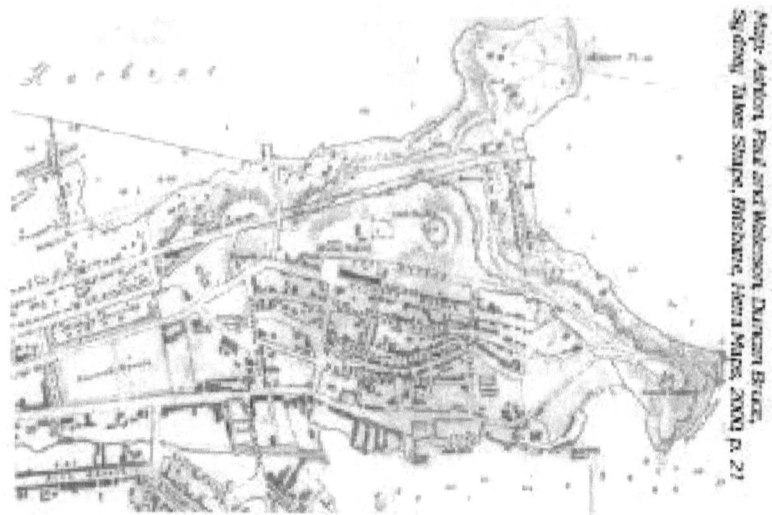

Map: Ashton, Paul and Waterson, Duncan Bruce, *Sydney Takes Shape*, Brisbane, Hema Maps, 2000, p. 21

1831 Map of the Town of Sydney showing the beginnings of wharfage in what is now Walsh Bay, Millers Point and Darling Harbour.

William was assigned to be a farm labourer in the area of Homebush. Serendipitously, his two good mates William Watts and George Davis also received the same assignment.

The farm owner was Thomas Laycock. He owned 500 acres where he ran sheep and cattle.

Laycock was a hard taskmaster. He provided inadequate food rations for the convicts and if he was displeased with one of his workers he was known to wield the cat freely. The convicts' quarters were freezing cold in winter and stifling hot in summer.

The three mates were locked in their huts. It was five degrees outside, and the hut had no form of heating. They cuddled up together to try and produce some body warmth.

'This is bloody ridiculous. I think we were better off on the hulk,' said Swallow.

'I agree we'd be better off trying to fend for ourselves in the bush,' said George.

'Do you reckon we could escape without being shot?' asked Watts.

'I think we could. I don't think they expect bolters out here.'

'So, do we all agree we make a run for it?' Swallow enquired.

'Yeah, why the fuck not.'

'When should we go?'

'Tomorrow after supper. It should be easier in the dark,' said Swallow.

'Right, I'm in,' said George.

'Me too,' said Willy.

The three convicts tried to get some sleep; none of them could, as there was too much on their minds.

The next morning, they were assigned to felling some large trees, cutting them up then splitting the logs to be used as firewood in the homestead so the Laycock family could be nice and warm while their convict labour froze.

The three comrades were counting down the hours until 5 pm when the workday concluded. They ate their supper of cold mutton and were due to be locked up for the night. They picked their moment when one of the guards was distracted and ran for their lives. The guards were unaware of the escape until final roll call. The alarm went out, a posse was assembled and ten men on horses set out to bring the escapees in.

The men ran until they couldn't take another step and then they dropped down, exhausted.

'What do you reckon? Do you think we got away with it?' asked William Watts.

'Who fucking knows? I suppose we'll find out soon enough. Let's try and get some sleep. I've got an idea it's going to be a long day tomorrow,' Swallow said.

Unbeknownst to the three escapees, the local aboriginal tribe, the Wann-gai, were on very friendly terms with Laycock. They became aware of the three convicts sleeping on their land. They reported back to Mr Laycock late that evening and led five armed men to the convicts' whereabouts.

The leader of the group was Laycock himself and once their quarry was spotted, the group surrounded the sleeping escapees.

'Wake up, you filthy scum. It's time to go home.'

They woke with a fright and immediately saw they were surrounded. They surrendered quietly.

They were marched back to Homebush and locked in a cell, which would normally hold one.

The next morning Laycock and an armed guard marched them into Sydney Town where the Magistrate would determine their fate.

After a day of marching, the convict group arrived at their destination, where they were interned in Darlinghurst Gaol on the town's fringe.

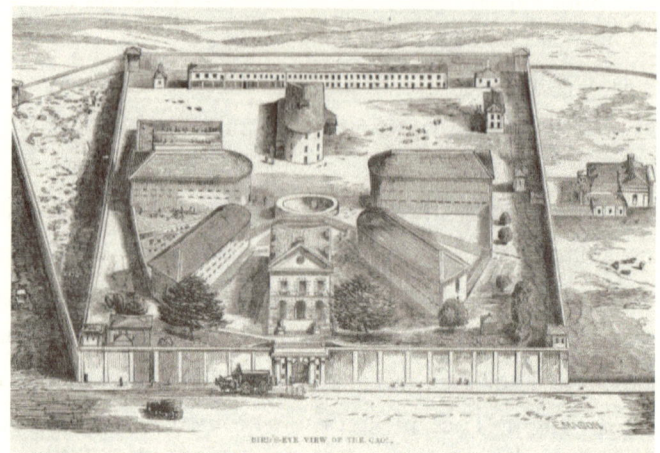

BIRD'S-EYE VIEW OF THE GAOL.

No time was wasted and the following morning the three prisoners were brought before Magistrate William Carter.

Magistrate Carter read the police report placed it down on his bench and ordered the prisoners to stand.

'You have committed a most serious crime and I have no hesitation in sentencing all of you to the maximum penalty.'

William Swallow whispered out the corner of his mouth, 'He's going to hang us.'

'You will be taken immediately from this place and receive 100 lashes each. You will then be transferred via ship to Sarah Island in Macquarie Harbour, Van Diemen's Land, where you shall remain for the term of your natural lives. Take them down.'

The three convicts were escorted back to Darlinghurst Gaol that same afternoon. They were tied to what convicts called "the three sisters", a wooden triangle.

They were flogged in concert, all receiving the 100th lash around about the same time.

They were dragged back to their cell to recover from the horrendous flogging.

'Are you all right Willy? What about you, George?'

'I'm fucking sore, mate. How could you not be after that?' said Willy.

'How are you faring, George?'

'I honestly thought I was going to die. I guess I'm all right now.'

How are you coping, William?' asked George.

'About the same as you two, I guess.'

'When do you think we'll be transferred to Sarah Island?'

'Who fucking knows. I'm not looking forward to it.'

'I've never heard of it,' said Willy.

'They say it's the worst of the fucking worst. You've got to have done something really bad to be sent there,' said William.

The three convicts, along with thirty other absconders and reoffenders, were transferred from Sydney Town to Hobart Town where they would board the *Cyprus* and sail to Macquarie Harbour and the infamous Sarah Island.

Sarah Island

Sarah Island penal settlement was established in 1827 just two years before William Swallow was due to arrive there. The population in 1829 comprised 100 military and about twelve civil servants. Some brought their wives and children.

The majority of the population was comprised of hardened convicts, approximately 350 in all.

These poor souls slept in the main petitionary in hammocks. Those convicts who were considered model prisoners slept in huts with up to eight men.

The most incorrigible convicts were relegated to Grummet Island, a most inhospitable place nicknamed "the island of despair". Here the convicts slept in a cold dormitory, more often than not in the same wet clothes they had been working in during the day.

Not all the labour was backbreaking. Some worked as carpenters, others as tanners and shoemakers.

The worst detail was allocated to new arrivals who would work in chains, hauling and piling logs which had been rafted up the Gordon River.

The administration showed some empathy for their charges; work would cease at midday on Saturday, and Sunday was a complete day of rest.

The rations arriving from Hobart Town were quite often inedible and had to be thrown away. Nevertheless, the rations received by each convict was:

1 lb 4 oz wheatmeal

1 lb fresh meat or salt beef

or 10 oz salt pork

11 oz salt

Each prisoner received their week's rations in bulk. It was up to each man to prepare and cook his food and ensure it lasted the entire week.

Vegetables were few and far between, and as a result, scurvy was rampant throughout the settlement.

Alcohol and tobacco were prohibited on the island, but, the military was active in the black market, therefore, prisoners could purchase both rum and tobacco for the right amount.

This was the environment William Swallow and the other mutineers were keen to avoid.

Sarah Island produced very little food, therefore, ships such as the *Cyprus* would bring in supplies. Also on board were 62 passengers including 31 convicts all in double irons and guarded by the 63rd Regiment under the command of Lieutenant Carew. His wife and two children accompanied him.

The ship set sail for her first port of call, Recherche Bay, and on arrival the captain concluded the winds were heading in the wrong direction to sail up the West Coast.

The captain decided it would be best to stay anchored in the bay until the winds became more favourable. However, the winds dropped altogether and the *Cyprus* remained becalmed.

The captain detailed the ship's doctor and a few men, including John Pobjoy, a convict, to catch some fish. Fresh fish was always welcome at the table.

Pobjoy was a short ugly man with bowlegs and bulbous eyes.

They lowered a small rowing boat and rowed some 300 yards away from the ship.

All seemed normal on board the brig. Five convicts were on the deck taking in the air, a normal practice. Three soldiers were supervising them and the remainder were below eating their evening meal.

One of the convicts nodded to his accomplice. This was the sign they had agreed upon to attack the guards. The five convicts attacked the guards, knocking them down to the deck. They were able to seize their weapons and hold them at bay. Two of the convicts grabbed a large hencoop and dragged it over the hatchway, preventing the soldiers from offering assistance to their fallen comrades. Other convicts were able to scramble onto the main deck and soon all had been released from their irons.

The captain heard the struggle from his cabin and rushed up to the deck. He had no sooner arrived when a convict smashed his face with the butt of a musket, knocking him unconscious.

A soldier down below fired his musket which achieved nothing apart from alerting the fishing expedition who began to row hurriedly back to the ship.

The convicts promised to spare the lives of the soldiers if they gave up their arms. A volley was the only answer they received, and two prisoners, on the convict ringleader Ferguson's directions, got buckets of boiling water from the galley and poured them down the hatchway. Panic-stricken by the knowledge that thirty desperate men were at liberty on the deck, and that the seizure of the vessel was only a matter of time, the scalded soldiers surrendered and passed up their arms.

It was getting dark and Lieutenant Carew and his fishing party were now alongside. They were told firmly to stand off.

'Men, do you really know what you are doing? Mutiny is a hanging offence and I can assure all of you - everybody will be caught. If you drop your weapons and return to your quarters I promise no mention of this incident will be made,' said Carew.

'Fuck off.'

'My wife and children are onboard. Can you assure me their safety?'

'Don't worry, they won't be harmed.

'Let me aboard so I can escort them to the beach on the boat.'

'You're not boarding this ship. Pobjoy will row you and ten others to shore. He'll continue until all are safely on shore.'

'Can I have my sword? It's very dear to my heart. My father used it during the battle of Waterloo.'

'No you can't. We need all the weapons we can muster. Now Pobjoy will row you to shore. Your wife and children will follow.'

Ferguson, the ringleader, called a muster asking for all who would follow him. All but thirteen convicts consented. The passengers and the thirteen were loaded into a longboat and landed with no shelter and very few provisions on the barren coast.

The provisions included 60 lbs. of biscuit, 20 lbs. of flour, 20 lbs. of sugar, 4 lbs. of tea, and 6 gals rum.

The *Cyprus* was almost ready to begin her adventure. William Swallow was voted in as the new master, based on his mariner and navigation skills. Ferguson was to be his lieutenant. He found a spare uniform of Lieutenant Carew's, and dressed appropriately for the entire voyage.

With provisions for six months for 400 men, arms, ammunition, and an experienced sailor as a captain, the mutineers felt that fortune had befriended them at last.

The mutineers sat down to a hearty supper and copious amounts of rum. The seventeen men discussed what should happen next. A few voted to sail to the Tahiti and settle there. Others voted for China, while others voted for India. A vote was taken and Tahiti was chosen. If any of the convicts wished to stay and settle, they could.

The men slept soundly apart from the guards on deck, who were there to ensure none of the marooned tried to take back the ship.

MAROONED

CHAPTER 4

The marooned passengers and soldiers did not enjoy their first night on shore at Recherche Bay. It was cold and extremely uncomfortable.

The group woke up to a clear morning. Lieutenant Carew looked out across the bay only to see the *Cyprus* in full sail heading out for the Pacific.

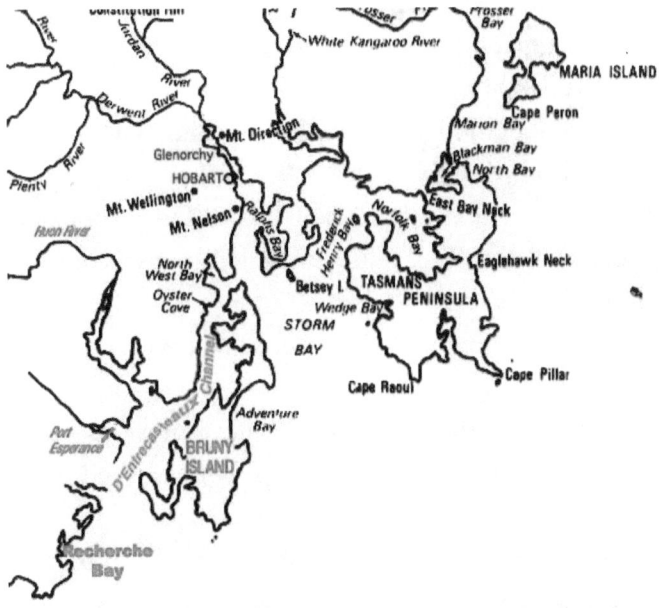

The group soon discovered the dire situation they were in; on one side they had the ocean with no means to navigate it, and on the other was the impenetrable scrub and finally impassable mountains. The meagre provisions would soon run out despite careful allocation to the forty people.

'I don't what's going to happen to us, mate. I can't believe we're in this situation. I blame the fucking captain. If he hadn't gone fishing, we would be in Macquarie Harbour by now,' said Private Arthur Dixon.

'I agree with you, mate, but there's no benefit in laying blame. We need to concentrate on how we can get out of this place. There's no way we can get to Sarah Island. I think our best bet is to go overland to Hobart Town,' said Corporal Francis Armstrong.

'That's easier said than done. You've seen how thick the bush is.'

'Well, it's got to be worth a try. Better than sitting on the beach hoping a ship might come along.'

'Or sitting on the beach waiting to die.'

The forty despondent souls became more and more depressed and most thought their destiny was to die in this remote place.

John Pobjoy, the convict who was on the fishing expedition, and his mate Andrew Morgan, overheard the conversation and approached Lieutenant Carew with a plan.

'Lieutenant, Andrew and I would like to try and walk to Hobart Town and organise a rescue,' said John.

'That's a very noble thought, lads, but I think you might be a little ambitious; the bush is impenetrable.'

'Sir, with respect, if we don't try we'll all be dead very soon.'

'Yes, I suppose you're right. If you're willing to try, who am I to stop you? When do you intend to leave?'

'It'll be tomorrow morning just after sunrise. We will need provisions, sir.'

'Yes, quite, I'll arrange some for you.'

The following morning the sky was red with a most magnificent sunrise. The two young men farewelled the group who wished them well and Godspeed.

The terrain made for slow going with not only the scrub to contend with but also many creek crossings. The lieutenant gave them a compass and instructed them to walk due north at all times.

It was impossible for Pobjoy and Morgan to determine how many miles they covered in the first day. All they knew was they were exhausted and their legs were aching.

'We've got some rum in our provisions, Andrew; let's have a sip or two.'

'Or three. It might help us sleep.'

'I don't think I'll need much help but yeah, why not? I think we've deserved it,' said John.

It wasn't quite what they were expecting the howling of Tasmanian devils and Tasmanian tigers constantly interrupted their sleep. They started off next morning, having eaten a meagre breakfast.

Recherche Bay

The going didn't get any easier on the second day but they reached a large river, the Huon, at the end of the day. This river was named after Jean-Michel Huon de Kermadec a French captain who was sent to try and find Jean-Francois de La Perouse who had disappeared.

'How in the hell are we going to cross this?'

'Can you swim?' asked Andrew.

'Aye.'

'I think we should strip off and tie our clothes around our heads. Then we can swim across, get dressed and be on our way.'

'That sounds like a reasonable plan.'

The two men were standing on the bank of the Huon, clothes wrapped around their heads like a turban, when they heard yelling.

'What the fuck is that?'

It was a group of Aboriginals, spears in hand, gesturing that they should retreat or they would attack.

The two men ran. Their clothes fell off their heads and were left behind and they didn't stop running for an hour, ensuring they were well out of range of the fierce warriors.

Finally, they sat down on a tree log and rested.

'What do we do now, mate? We're totally naked in the bush.'

'There's not much else we can do, Andrew. We'll have to return to the camp.'

WE ARE SAILING

CHAPTER 5

Captain Swallow and his crew were heading for the north island of New Zealand. It was not their intention to stay there as, after all, it was a British colony. His plan was to sail between the north and south islands to ensure the *Cyprus* stayed away from the normal shipping lanes.

Captain Swallow intended to pick up the prevailing winds, which would take the *Cyprus* to Tahiti.

Swallow knew that without any rules the ship's crew would run riot and the *Cyprus* would descend into anarchy.

With the help of his lieutenant, he comprised a set of rules, which were to be obeyed without compromise.

1. Every man shall have an equal vote on all matters pertaining to the voyage.
2. All men will be entitled to fresh provisions and rum while the provisions last.
3. If another ship is encountered and a decision is made by the crew to pirate it; the prize will be divided equally.
4. If any man steals from another he will have his ears removed and be set ashore at the first opportunity.
5. Gambling on board of any type is strictly forbidden.
6. All crew shall keep their weapons clean and functionally ready for action.
7. All crew are to wash every day and maintain their personal hygiene.

Captain Swallow and Lieutenant Ferguson were satisfied that their rules should ensure a safe passage.

After one day sailing Swallow took Captain's Waldron's sexton from his cabin; an instrument that would later ensure his freedom.

At noon he took the measurements, which would tell him the latitude of the ship. With this instrument, Swallow would navigate the pirates' route through the Pacific and beyond.

'How the fuck can you tell with that thing where the hell we are?' asked Ferguson.

'It's a bit complicated, mate. I was trained to use it by a very experienced navigator.'

'Well, as long as you know what you're doing, mate, we should find the Tahiti without a problem.'

'Have no fear, Ferguson, we'll be there before you know it.'

'Good. I hear the women are something to behold.'

'So that's why you voted for the Tahiti. You're after some Bread and Butter.'

'Bloody oath, William, it's been a few years.'

'Yeah, me too.'

'I've been thinking we really should change the name of the brig. Every British vessel will be looking for us,' added Captain Swallow.

'I suppose you're right. We should remove the figurehead too. She will make us stand out.'

'You're right— we should.'

'We are close to the Bay of Islands according to my charts.'

Captain Swallow set his course for the safe haven where the crew could remove the figurehead and rename the ship to *Friends*.

The work took the best part of the day. It was agreed by the crew that they remain anchored until first light when they would continue their voyage across the Pacific.

'A few of the men have requested they take the longboat and see if they catch some fish, Captain,' said Ferguson.

'I don't see why not. It will probably be the last chance we have for quite a while.'

'You never know… we might have fresh fish for supper.'

'Yes, it would make a nice change from the rations we've been eating.'

Four of the crew, Lynch, Pennell, Towers and Templeton, lowered the boat and began rowing away from the ship. The sea was calm and their hopes were high. When they reached a suitable distance from the newly renames *Friends*, they lowered their lines. The only bait they could muster was some dried mutton and bread.

It was Towers who caught the first fish. It was a skipjack tuna, a large fish much sought after by the Maori people. Next, Templeton snagged a kingfish.

A kahawai was the next fish caught by Lynch. After two hours of fishing in the Bay of Islands, the four men had caught over thirty fish; the crew would feast that night.

The fishing expedition brought their catch back to the ship. All were right proud of their efforts and keen to cook up a sailors' banquet.

Every crewmember ate his fair share, knowing it would be sometime before they tasted fish again.

After supper, Captain Swallow asked Lieutenant Ferguson to come to his cabin as he had some issues he wanted to discuss.

'Ferguson, I'm concerned about the discipline on this ship. If we are to make it to our desired destination, we need to ensure every member of the crew is pulling his weight. There are tasks to perform... not the least being always having a man on watch, not drinking rum down below. We are very vulnerable. For all we know; half the British Navy is looking for us.

'From now on, six shifts of four hours each will be maintained. Each of the nineteen crew will be required to stand watch in their turn.'

'I'll arrange for the first shift tonight, Captain.'

'Excellent, now the other thing I wish to discuss with you is how we can keep the crew busy throughout the day. If we permit them to lie about all day we'll have serious trouble to contend with.

'My time in the Navy taught me that the sailors needed to be occupied washing the decks, mending sails and so on.'

'I see what you mean, Captain. I'll arrange for a work roster immediately.'

A daily routine was established and adhered to for the remainder of the voyage.

The Cyprus aka *Friends of Boston* became a regimented ship, not dissimilar to a ship in the Royal Navy although these sailors had very little experience.

Swallow knew if there was little discipline the chances of survival were low.

The crew accepted the new regime with very little complaint. Swallow knew that he could lose his captaincy at any time; it would take only a vote by the men to oust him. He also knew that without his navigation skills the ship would be at risk.

Captain Swallow set his course for Tahiti. He was aware that the *Bounty*'s mutineers lived on this idyllic island for five months in 1788. He hoped for the same friendly treatment from the Tahitians that the *Bounty* crew received, particularly from the women.

NAKED WE STAND
NAKED WE FALL

CHAPTER 6

The weather was inclement, heavy rain was falling and the temperature was eight degrees Celsius. These conditions were not conducive to scrambling through the Tasmanian bush.

'John, I'm fucking freezing. What are we going to do?'

'Nothing much we can do, Andrew, except keep moving. It took us two days to reach the big river. I estimate we have another day and a half to reach the camp and some warm clothes and a campfire.'

'Who's going to give us clothes?'

'It'll be fine. I know some of them brought their bags with them when they came ashore.'

'It's getting dark, mate. We better make camp and head off early tomorrow morning.'

'I wish I had my matches. I had a box in my trousers pocket. We certainly could do with a fire right now,' said John.

'True, although even if we had matches we'd be hard-pressed to find some dry wood,' said Andrew.

'Andrew… do you see what I see?'

'What do you mean?'

'I think that's a cave in that cliff face.'

'Bloody hell, I think you're right! I hope there isn't any Tasmanian Tigers in there.'

'Well, I for one am going in there. Anything to be out of this fucking rain.'

'I'm with you, mate. Hold on— wait for me.'

The two men entered the cave. There was still enough light to see if they were sharing it with a tiger or a devil, but they weren't.

They were delighted to discover dry grass, possibly from some sort of nest. This would serve as a blanket. What they didn't know was the aboriginals had used this cave for shelter for many thousands of years. They were out of the weather and had some warmth. Things were looking up.

The two men had a fitful sleep, but at least they did sleep.

The next morning brought with it clear skies. It was still cold but at least it wasn't raining.

On empty stomachs, the men headed out, hoping to reach the camp by nightfall. It continued to be tough going. The bush was creating lacerations on their naked bodies, and as a result, both men looked as if they had received a flogging from the cat o' nine tails.

At 4 pm they walked into the camp. The other marooned passengers looked at them in horror. Lieutenant Carew whisked them away to clean them up and find some suitable clothes.

Once that was achieved, the lieutenant called everybody together to hear about the adventures of Morgan and Pobjoy.

Everybody, including Lieutenant Carew, was extremely disappointed to hear the adventurers' tale of woe.

The feeling among the group was one of despair. They would all die of starvation.

TAHITI SOUNDS NICE

CHAPTER 7

The Bounty
December 1787

The *Bounty* left England for Tahiti in the South Pacific, where it was to collect a cargo of breadfruit saplings to transport to the West Indies. There, the breadfruit would become the staple food for slaves. After a 10-month journey, the *Bounty* arrived in Tahiti in October 1788 and remained there for more than five months. On Tahiti, the crew enjoyed an idyllic life, revelling in the comfortable climate, lush surroundings, sexually liberated women and the famous hospitality of the Tahitians. Fletcher Christian fell in love with a Tahitian woman named Mauatua.

On April 4, 1789, the *Bounty* departed Tahiti with its store of breadfruit saplings. On April 28, near the island of Tonga, Christian and 25 petty officers and seamen seized the ship.

The crew of the *Bounty* was greeted with dozens of canoes paddling out to meet the ship. The Tahitian men were paddling furiously while the Tahitian girls, all topless, were waving frantically.

The sea-weary sailors had a wonderful time with the ever-willing women of the island.

The crew of the *Cyprus* aka *Friends of Boston* were hoping for the same reception.

The sea was fair for the first twenty days, and the crew were enjoying the sunshine despite still having their daily tasks to perform. They found time to sit on the deck smoking their pipes, using the tobacco they stole from the supplies, and talked about their future lives.

On the twenty-first day, things aboard the *Friends of Boston* changed.

'Captain, those clouds look a bit ominous. Do you think we're in for a storm?'

'I don't think we're in for a storm, Ferguson. I fucking know it.'

'What should we do?'

'Tell the men to lower all the sails bar the foremast and make sure they're quick about it. I don't think we have much time.'

Captain Swallow could see the waves were getting bigger. Seawater was beginning to wash over the decks and the crew were having trouble maintaining their balance. An experienced crew would have lowered the sails quick time, but, the *Friends of Boston'* inexperienced crew were taking forever. At last the sails had been lowered. Captain Swallow felt more at ease although he knew they could easily end up a shipwreck.

Friends of Boston was doing her best, as was the crew, but the waves were now above the deck. Objects that had not been secured were being washed overboard.

One crewmember, John Brown, was washed overboard. Every man on board knew he would drown, but there was nothing they could do.

For the next twenty-four hours nobody on board the brig slept or ate. They spent all their energy staying alive.

Finally, the storm abated and the seas were calm with favourable winds to take them to their destination.

Despite losing momentum during the storm, *Friends of Boston* would arrive in Tahiti in twelve days.

The convicts were finding the life of freedom was not what it was cracked up to be. They discovered it was hard work and this combined with constant thirst, sunburn and other general discomforts, made life difficult.

In crossing the Pacific they encountered three cyclonic storms and they were fortunate to lose only one man. They were all looking forward to the calm waters of Tahiti, and to leaving the mountainous seas, howling winds and the frightening thunder and lightning storms behind them.

This was not the only thing causing discontent among the crew. A mistrust of Captain Swallow's intentions in navigating the ship began to spread throughout the men.

'Captain Swallow— permission to enter your cabin.'

'Come in, Ferguson. What's on your mind?'

'We, that is Herring, Jones and Pennell and I, would like you to explain how the charts and logs work.'

'Why? Are you thinking of taking over the navigation of the ship?'

'No, but we all believe we should be in Tahiti by now. You said at the beginning of the voyage it would take thirty days.'

'I didn't take into account that we would encounter three cyclonic storms.'

'Yeah, I suppose there was that.'

'If you would like me to stand down, lads, I'd be more than happy to do so.'

'No, no… it's just that we would like to know what's happening.'

'I see well I'll try and explain things better.'

That wasn't the end of the matter; arguments occurred regularly.

The mutineers were becoming mutinous again, but they knew Swallow was the only person who could navigate.

William went out on deck at noon. As usual, he took his measurements and announced by his reckoning the brig was 50 nautical miles to the westward of Tahiti. This caused great excitement among the crew. It was late afternoon when the yell went out 'Land Ho!' The next call was 'Ho! Tahiti Ho!'

The distinctive mountain peaks confirmed it. The ship of fools had crossed the Pacific to paradise.

The crew were champing at the bit to meet the beautiful island women who had a reputation for abandoned lovemaking.

They heard the reports about the *Bounty* arriving and the fun and frivolity the crew enjoyed and they were all looking forward to the same friendly treatment.

Captain Swallow navigated the ship into Matavai Bay; the same bay the *Bounty* sailed into all those years before.

The crew were all at the ship's railing waving to the thirty odd canoes being paddled towards the *Friends of Boston*. As the canoes got closer, the crew could see there were no women, just ferocious looking warriors with spears and spiked clubs. It was clear the *Friends of Boston* was not welcome.

Captain Swallow took advantage of the strong south-easterly and headed back out to sea.

Ferguson and the other ringleaders approached Swallow.

'So what in the fuck do we do now, Swallow?'

'It's Captain Swallow. We need to find another island. Our fresh water is almost depleted.'

'Have you got any idea where we should head?'

'I do, the Friendly Islands…Tonga.'

'How far is it?'

'About twelve hundred miles to the west with favourable winds so we could be there in a week.'

'That sounds all right, I can't believe we sailed for thirty-six days or whatever it was and we can't even anchor off the island. It's just not good enough, Captain Swallow.'

'Don't tell me you're blaming me for not landing on Tahiti. I know you blame me for everything that goes wrong on this ship but don't blame me for the inhospitable welcome.'

How to Build a Coracle

Chapter 8

Morgan and Pobjoy approached Lieutenant Carew with a plan they believed would work.

'Lieutenant, we've been thinking how we can escape this Godforsaken place and get back to Hobart Town.'

'Well?'

'We build a boat and two of us sail back to Hobart Town and alert the authorities to our situation. They would then dispatch a ship to rescue us.'

'You propose to build a boat? May I ask what with?'

'Have you ever heard of a coracle?'

'No, I haven't. I take it that is some sort of a boat?'

'Yes, sir; the Irish and Welsh both use them.'

Two Man Coracle

'So, how does one go about constructing a coracle?'

'Sir, we need willows, canvas, tar, nails and some tools.'

'Well, I haven't seen too many willows growing around here as for the canvas that was used for the *Cyprus*'s sails and as you know, she's long gone. Where are you going to source tar, nails and tools? I suggest God only knows.'

'Sir, I know I can do it. I've done my research. There are plenty of green sticks that can be bent to the right shape and they would be just as supple as willow.

'What about the nails?'

We can lash the sticks rather than nail them. I know some of the seamen brought twine with them when they came ashore.'

'So that still leaves you with a lack of canvas. How are you going to overcome that problem?'

'Sir, some of the soldiers under your command brought hammocks ashore. They would be perfect.'

'That's all well and good, Morgan, but we need to sew it.'

'One of the soldiers brought sail-needles.'

'I must admit it's looking more promising. We don't have any tar or tools and that presents a problem.'

'I believe some of the men have beeswax and soap that would make a great substitute for tar.'

'I have asked around and have discovered we have three pocketknives among the group. I suggest we use gum from the gum-trees which would also help eliminate the tar problem,' said Pobjoy.

'So, you can guarantee me this thing will float?'

'Absolutely, sir. Coracles have been used for many hundreds of years.

May I suggest Pobjoy and I head down the coast and into the Derwent? We should make it in four days. It would have to be better than the overland trip we undertook,' said Morgan.

'Give it a try. We don't have too many other options. Take the hammocks and wax and anything else you need. Please make haste because we don't have much time.'

Morgan seconded a dozen men to go into the scrub to find green tea-tree and wattle stems. They needed to be straight and thin and about ten feet in length. This is what they would use to build the frame of the coracle.

Within the hour, thirty or more sticks were laid out on the sandy ground and stripped of leaves and twigs. Morgan inspected the sticks, choosing a particularly strong one for the keel.

Morgan lashed the sticks together to form the shape of the coracle. The next and most difficult step was to cover the frame with canvas. The soldiers relinquished their hammocks for the good of the cause.

Mrs Carew offered her services as a seamstress and pattern maker and she also offered a pair of dressmaking scissors to cut the canvas.

The canvas was stretched over the frame and sewed expertly by Morgan and Mrs Carew.

The final task was to seal the canvas with the concoction they had mixed as a substitute for tar.

Once that task was achieved, the coracle was left to dry until the next day.

The penultimate step was to melt the remainder of the wax and add the soap and then apply the sticky mixture onto the canvas hull with a paintbrush made from wattle brush.

The final step was to melt the gum from eucalyptus and wattle trees and apply it as a varnish.

Morgan then arranged for two of the castaways to whittle some round branches into paddles. They also carved some seats for the two boatmen.

All was ready for the launching.

However, there was discontent brewing among the convict castaways.

'There's no fucking way that straw boat will make it to Hobart Town,' said the convict Parsons.

'Yeah, I'm with you, mate. We'd have a much better chance going overland,' said Hall.

'Hold on, matey. They already tried that and didn't even cross the Huon River let alone get to Hobart Town,' said Fletcher.

'Yeah, but who did they send? The two twats who built the fucking boat. I'm sure they wanted to build the thing well before they set off on their adventure,' said Parsons.

'Why don't we approach the lieutenant and suggest the five of us go overland just in case the boat doesn't make it?' suggested Hall.

'Fair enough.'

A deputation of three convicts and two sailors requested a meeting with the officers on Sunday morning and it was granted.

'Our proposal is we travel through the forest, not the shore. This route would enable us to go around the head of the Huon.'

Lieutenant Carew was not keen. If these men lost their way and perished or if they were attacked and killed by the natives or worse still absconded and became bushrangers, he would be blamed.

'I'll consider your proposal, but let's first see if the coracle floats. Dismissed.'

He conferred with Doctor Williams and Captain Harrison.

'In my opinion, we should allow the overland party to proceed. I believe an overland party would have a much better chance of success rather than this crazy notion that this little boat made of twigs could sail proudly into Hobart Town and save us all.'

'I trust Morgan and Pobjoy, but I don't trust a group of convicts without supervision trekking through the forest,' said Lieutenant Carew.

'Does it really matter if they abscond or perish? You've already lost nineteen convicts and no doubt you'll be court-martialled for that. If the convicts are successful you may retrieve your position,' said Doctor Williams.

'I hear what you're saying, doctor, and I acknowledge that in all likelihood I will be court-martialled. What would make it worse would be losing nineteen convicts, plus another five plus Morgan and Pobjoy.

'It would make it even worse for your reputation if everyone here dies of starvation. We only have a few days rations left.'

'What do you think, Captain?'

'I have no doubt the coracle will float and as long as they enjoy calm weather they have a better than even chance they will make it to Hobart Town. However, if she encounters rough seas, she will founder and sink.'

'How long do you think she would take to make Hobart Town?'

'Depending on the tides and currents… a week. She may meet up with a ship in the D'Entrecasteaux Channel if she is fortunate.'

So what do you recommend, Captain?'

'I think the coracle should be sent from here as soon as possible. Having said that, the overland party should be sent as well.'

'Thank you, Captain.'

'Lieutenant, I will support you if you are court-martialled.'

'Thank you once again, sir.'

'Well, that's agreed. We dispatch the overland party tomorrow but not before we see the coracle float.'

'One more thing, Carew. I think we should write a letter to be carried by the two groups to the Superintendent at Birches Bay explaining our predicament.'

'I agree, Doctor. I will write it tonight.'

To the Superintendent,

Birches Bay,

Dear sir,

These will inform you that the brig Cyprus has been captured by the prisoners, who sent us together with family, soldiers, and sailors; in all forty persons, on shore. We have been here nine days and are without provisions. Your immediate assistance will be the cause of saving us from starvation.

The men who bear this have behaved in an exemplary manner and of course will be treated accordingly.

We beg to remain

dear sir,

your obedient servants.

W.M. Carew, Lieu 63rd Regiment

Walter Williams, Surgeon

Robert Harrison Captain

P.S. Four of the soldiers are severely wounded

Doctor Williams refused to sign the letter as the injuries were highly exaggerated.

The doctor wrapped the letters in canvas and stitched with twine.

'Doctor Williams, Captain, shall we inspect the vessel on the beach?' said Carew.

Morgan and Pobjoy were waiting next to the coracle, which was resting on the water's edge.

''She's ready to go,' shouted Morgan.

All the castaways were on the beach; some hopeful, some despondent, waiting for the launch.

Morgan and Pobjoy moved the vessel into the water and boarded, while two members of the group held her steady and then pushed her out. The two men began paddling and continued for fifteen minutes albeit close to the shore.

Once they were satisfied with her seaworthiness they brought the coracle back to shore. They lifted her gently on to the sand.

'I told you it would float like a duck, sir.'

'That you did, Morgan, that you did,' said a much-relieved lieutenant.

'It is dry as a bone inside, sir; she's watertight.'

The marooned group began to clap the two proud boat builders.

What lay ahead of the two men was forty miles along the shore to the mouth of the Derwent. When they left the safe haven of Recherche Bay they would have to navigate ten miles of ocean seas and strong currents before entering D'Entrecasteaux Channel.

A small container of drinking water and a few days' provisions were loaded into the coracle. Their boots and a canvas shelter were also loaded.

'We'll be on our way while the weather is calm. I can navigate by the stars,' said Pobjoy.

Lieutenant Carew pulled the two men aside.

'You know you are not compelled to go, don't you?'

'Yes, sir, but we have very little choice and besides, we have to beat the land crew,' said Pobjoy.

' If we both die so be it. We'll die here soon anyway,' said Morgan.

'Good men, off you go and Godspeed.'

Doctor Williams tied the canvas bag containing the letters around Pobjoy's neck.

The captain called out for three cheers and the castaways responded enthusiastically.

The two men one; a Welshman the other a Cockney, stepped into the fragile boat and headed out of the bay and into the open ocean.

The thirty-eight castaways stayed on the beach until the coracle and the two men were out of sight. Their last hopes rested on their success.

Two Men and a Coracle

Chapter 9

Woodcut dated 1829 of Morgan and Pobjoy building the coracle

Once the two sailors left the safe haven of Recherche Bay, the seas became quite rough, tossing the coracle about like a child's toy. The captain had given them a tobacco container for the purpose of baling out water. It was getting much use. Still the little homemade vessel bobbed and swayed but nevertheless stayed afloat. They were making headway, and that was the most important thing.

'Andrew, do you see what I see?'

'No, where abouts?'

'To the south I see lights. It could be the navigation lights of a ship, the *Georgiana* more than likely.'

'Ship ahoy! Ship ahoy!' they both yelled at the top of their voices.

'Fuck it it's no use; they're too far away and they can't hear us,' said Pobjoy

'If we'd launched an hour or two earlier she may have seen us.'

'I reckon there have been ships passing by Recherche Bay since we were out on the beach,' said Morgan.

'You're probably right but we wouldn't know, would we?'

'If the so-called lieutenant moved us all to the headland, we may have been sighted by passing ships. He's done fuck all apart from bemoaning our predicament. It wasn't him who decided we should try to reach Hobart Town by land; it was us two. It wasn't him who came up with the idea to build a coracle and alert the authorities of our plight; it was us. We had to talk the bastard into letting us build the fucking thing for God's sake.'

'I thought Captain Harrison might have intervened and moved the group,' said Pobjoy.

'You've got to be kidding. That drunk wouldn't be able to decide where he'd have his next piss,' said Morgan.

'Do you reckon we'll earn a pardon from our heroic efforts?' asked Pobjoy.

'I wouldn't hold out for it. These bastards don't hand them out too often. How much time have you got, John?'

'I've only got another eighteen months; how about you?'

'Not much more than you; life.'

Neither man got any sleep on their first night at sea, but that didn't deter them.

'I tell you what, mate, I can't see myself getting in a boat again for quite a while,' said Andrew Morgan.

'I know what you mean, although I wouldn't mind boarding s ship to take me home to England.'

'You don't think we should escape while we have the chance?'

'No, mate, we have a duty to deliver the letter and save the castaways at Recherche Bay.'

'You're right. Just a thought.'

'We don't seem to be making much headway. That headland seems about as far from us as it did a couple of hours ago.'

'I'm afraid the ebb tide is against us so we're paddling against a strong current,' said Morgan.

'When do you reckon we should beach her and take a break?' asked Pobjoy.

'Not until daylight. It would be too dangerous at night and we could damage the coracle.'

The two convicts continued to paddle hard throughout the night, and at last, they could see the sunrise. They spotted a small island, Partridge Island, at the tip of Bruny Island and they paddled furiously and made the beach, exhausted.

They lit a fire and ate some of the measly provisions they were given. They then slept for several hours. Morgan woke to observe the masts and rigging of a ship.

The two men quickly packed up their things and launched the coracle, heading for the ship they hoped would be their salvation.

The seas were rough which was probably the reason the barque laid anchor off Partridge Island.

'I hope she doesn't pull up anchor before we reach her,' said Pobjoy.

'I can't see her setting sail in these conditions. I'm sure she will remain anchored until tomorrow.'

'Do you think we're making headway?'

'I'm sure we are. Just keep paddling as hard as you can. This is our big opportunity.'

After three hours, the coracle was within shouting distance of the three-masted ship.

'Ship ahoy!' they yelled at the tops of their voices.

'Identify yourselves,' was the response from the ship.

'We are two seamen in distress.'

'Bring your boat alongside.'

Several sailors were looking down at the two men in their strange looking vessel. They were suspicious of their motives.

Captain Hudson thought these two could be escaped convicts from Birches Bay.

'Who are you?' Captain Hudson shouted.

The ship turned out to be the *Orelia,* bound for the newly established settlement on the Swan River in Western Australia. She was carrying foodstuffs and other supplies for the inhabitants.

'If you are convicts attempting to escape I will not let you aboard.'

'We were on board the brig *Cyprus* when pirates seized her.'

'Are you serious?'

'Indeed we are, sir.'

'All right, come aboard and bring your strange boat with you.'

Several seamen attached a rope to the coracle and hauled it on board. The ship's crew were fascinated by its construction.

Andrew and John were given blankets and food. They were absolutely exhausted.

The crew of the *Orelia* were fascinated by the story the two men told. They heard of the seizure of the *Cyprus,* the castaways near starvation and how Morgan and Pobjoy constructed the coracle and how they paddled fifteen miles in rough seas from Recherche Bay to Partridge Island.

Next morning, Captain Hudson ordered the two longboats to be launched. The first mate was in charge of the first boat, taking essential provisions to the castaways at Recherche Bay.

The second longboat took Pobjoy and Morgan to Birches Bay to deliver the message.

It took only a few hours for both boats to reach their destinations.

Lieutenant Carew was sitting on the beach lamenting about the situation he found himself in. He had lost the *Cyprus* to convict pirates; the castaways were near starvation despite the mussel soup they were served each day, and there was no doubt in his mind that he would be court-marshalled if he ever did leave this Godforsaken bay.

As he looked out to sea with his morose contemplations omnipresent in his mind, he noticed a boat under sail heading for the bay. He jumped up and began waving his arms. The occupants of the longboat acknowledged his presence with waving and shouting. The boat reached the shore and the eight men aboard greeted the lieutenant, informing him it was Pobjoy and Morgan who were responsible for their rescue.

By this time the other castaways had congregated on the beach laughing and crying, shouting and kneeling in quiet prayer.

The crew from the *Orelia* began to unload the provisions they had brought with them. Pickled pork, biscuits and other essential items were enough for the next few days at least.

The camp now knew their rescue was imminent, with the knowledge that Morgan and Pobjoy completed their mission. A ship from Hobart Town would arrive at Recherche Bay any day.

'We won't abandon you. Rest assured, the *Orelia* will remain anchored until we are sure you have all been rescued,' said the first mate.

The spirit of the occupants of the camp was high. At last, a rescue!

UNGRATEFUL SODS

CHAPTER 10

Morgan and Pobjoy arrived at Birches Bay under full sail in the second longboat.

The gentleman in charge of the convicts and soldiers at Birches Bay was a man called Munro. Morgan handed him the letter penned by the captain of the *Cyprus*, Captain Harrison.

Munro questioned Morgan and Pobjoy for some time before agreeing to their request that they take the letter to Hobart Town post haste.

The *Orelia's* longboat was used to ferry the two men and their important message to Hobart Town. Upon arrival, the letter was passed on to Governor Arthur for his perusal. Having digested its contents he ordered the *Opossum* to sail immediately to Recherche Bay.

The *Opossum* arrived at Recherche Bay later the same day. The two longboats and their crew returned to the *Orelia*.

She then set sail for Western Australia on her original mission.

The heroes' welcome Pobjoy and Morgan were expecting didn't eventuate. Instead, they were both interned in Hobart Gaol, in irons. The only consolation was that they shared a cell; albeit cold, dark and damp.

Governor Arthur suspected both of them were involved in the mutiny and had absconded.

'What the fuck is going on here, Morgan? We put our lives at risk so that we could save thirty-three men, women and children who we know would have perished if it wasn't for our actions, and now the pricks have put us in irons and locked us up.'

'Don't ask me, Pobjoy. It's obvious they don't trust us. Once a convict always a convict.'

'And I thought I would receive a full pardon, what a load of rubbish.'

The *Opossum* sailed into Recherche Bay and weighed anchor a hundred yards offshore. The captain ordered the longboats to be lowered and several crewmembers rowed the two boats ashore.

The castaways were ecstatic, albeit weak from camping out with few provisions for thirteen nights. When all were aboard, the *Opossum* set sail for Hobart Town where she arrived the following morning.

Hobart Town 1830

There was jubilation on the dock as the residents of Hobart Town had learned of the perilous adventure the day before from a newspaper article in the *Hobart Town Courier*.

The seven convicts who refused to join the pirates and had contributed to the survival of the group were placed in chains and incarcerated with Pobjoy and Morgan.

Governor Arthur sent another ship, the *Derwent*, to Macquarie Harbour with provisions. The convicts and the garrison were perilously short of provisions as a result of the loss of the *Cyprus*.

When the *Derwent* arrived, the situation was dire. The population of Sarah Island was at starvation level, surviving on the odd wallaby the guards were lucky enough to shoot.

Back at Recherche Bay, the five convicts that set out on a rescue mission were missing. It had been a week since they departed and the authorities were concerned that they had perished in the bush.

Munro from Birches Bay was ordered to dispatch a search party up the Huon River in the hope of finding them.

On Friday, September 4, the search party sighted the five bedraggled convicts on the riverbank. It was obvious they were all extremely fatigued.

'My name is Fletcher, and I was sent to find you all. Are you all right?'

'No, we're not all right. We haven't eaten for two days,' said Gould.

'How long did it take you to reach here?'

'Too bloody long. I think it was seven days. That's why we don't have any food left.'

'Is anybody injured?'

'Yeah, Briggs received a flesh wound from a native's spear.'

'You were attacked by natives?'

'Yeah, the bastards bailed us up when we reached the Huon.'

'Which one of you is Briggs?'

'I am.'

'Are you all right?'

'Yeah, I'll survive.'

'Right, well let's get some food into you and get you to Hobart Town.'

The five men and the crew from the longboat sailed up the Derwent River and into the dock at Hobart Town.

On arrival, they were fettered in chains and incarcerated with the others.

Pobjoy lay in his cold dank cell along with Morgan and the five convicts that became the land mission.

'Surely when they discover what we all did to save the castaways they'll release us from this fucking cell,' said Morgan.

'Who knows they may want to keep us undercover from the public. You know, not admit that they lost the *Cyprus* and nearly lost thirty-three souls down south,' said Pobjoy.

'I don't think so. There's already been an article printed in *Hobart Town Courier*. The whole fucking town knows by now,' said Morgan.

As the days passed, Pobjoy became more and more disheartened at the treatment he and the other convicts were receiving. His health suffered terribly until he could no longer rise from his bed.

'Come on, matey. We'll be all right; you just wait and see— the governor will pardon us all. You've got to keep your spirits up,' said Morgan.

The authorities allowed the melancholic convict to make a statement petitioning the Sheriff of Hobart Gaol. He was allocated a clerk to record his statement as he was illiterate.

September 7

Pobjoy described his actions on the day of the mutiny.

'As a seaman, I was permitted to work on the deck of the *Cyprus*. I refused to join the mutineers and joined the rest of the passengers and soldiers on the beach at Recherche Bay.

'Morgan and I made two attempts to bring rescue to the castaways; the first attempt across the land was unsuccessful. Natives attacked us and we lost our clothes. By the time we reached camp we were battered and bruised.

'Soon after we returned to camp, Morgan and I devised a plan to find help via water.'

Pobjoy explained how they constructed the coracle and delivered the letter to the Captain of the *Orelia* and in turn to Governor Arthur, facilitating the rescue of the castaways.

His concluding paragraph read… 'Your Petitioner has submitted this account to you praying Your Honour will be good enough to take his late suffering into your humane consideration. I have now only eighteen months to serve out of fourteen years and all the hardships and sufferings that I have undergone was for the good of the sufferers generally.

'At my return to Hobart Town, I was sent to gaol loaded with chains in a weak state of body, which my late sufferings occasioned. I have been under the necessity of keeping my bed.

'What I have stated is the truth and will be corroborated by the Officer and the Doctor.

'Your Honour's attention will oblige your most obedient and humble servant.

'John Pobjoy' X

Governor Arthur was sitting at his Huon pine desk in his study. He thought it ironic that this magnificent timber was felled and milled at Sarah Island before being transported to Hobart Town and fashioned into a magnificent desk designed by John Lee Archer.

He now had to decide if the *Cyprus* convicts being held in captivity be sent to Sarah Island or elsewhere.

It had been five weeks since the Recherche Bay rescue. Most of the castaways had resumed their normal lives, but not so the thirteen convicts who refused to take part in the mutiny.

Finally, after much research and interviewing all who were involved, Governor Arthur made the decision to discharge twelve of the thirteen convicts from gaol.

John Pobjoy was the only one of the twelve who received a full pardon having served over twelve years of his original fourteen-year sentence.

The remainder had their sentences of transportation to Macquarie Island revoked.

Morgan, being a lifer, was given no such privileges. He served out his sentence as a seaman on Government vessels around Tasmania.

Only one of the thirteen remained in gaol. He was John Hall, who admitted to taking up arms on the deck of the *Cyprus*. He had been sentenced to hang, but Governor Arthur took into consideration his involvement in the attempted land rescue. He was dispatched back to Sarah Island to complete his sentence.

THE FRIENDLY ISLES

CHAPTER 11

Swallow had the decision *Friends of Boston* aka *Cyprus* would sail to the Friendly Isles aka Tonga if they could not anchor in Matavai Bay. He just had to convince the crew.

The relationship between Captain Swallow and Lieutenant Ferguson was anything but good, but they both knew they needed to cooperate with each other or anarchy would descend on the ship.

In an altercation soon after they left the waters off Tahiti, Captain Swallow resigned suggesting Ferguson be elected Captain.

'Muster all hands; it's time to elect a new captain. I've had enough. My suggestion would be Ferguson. He seems to think he could take you into port. I'm afraid I failed.

'Yes, he thinks it will be plain sailing and only thirty miles away. What I can tell you is that in this wind and current with an inexperienced crew she'll have to sail thirty miles on tacks to make five miles headway in a day, but she'll drift away from the island and she'll be back where you all started.'

I don't want to be fucking captain,' said Ferguson.

'Any other suggestions, mates?'

No man spoke.

'So, I'm still captain. I'll try to get us into Matavai Bay tomorrow morning, but make no mistake, it will be fucking hard work and every man must pull his weight. If we do make it into the bay there could well be a British warship waiting to greet us or Tahitian warriors who don't want us near.'

Ferguson and Swallow shook hands and drank a tot of brandy together. Things were back to normal.

The next morning, Captain Swallow rose and headed straight for the poop deck to ascertain the direction and strength of the wind. The south -easterly had strengthened.

All hands were called out to shake out and raise the sails Swallow directed the work from the poop.

Soon *Cyprus* was working to windward on a starboard tack in choppy seas.

As the sun became hotter, so did the crew. Sweat was pouring down their faces and backs but these men were not sailors and each time Swallow ordered to tack, the brig missed the tack.

No matter what Captain Swallow tried, it failed, so he called a halt for lunch where the crew were fed healthy portions of salted pork, biscuits and tea.

The crew discussed their predicament over their lunch.

'Blimey, I don't know how much harder we can work. No matter how much we try nothing's good enough for Swallow,' said Jones.

'Come on, he's doing his best to get us to Tahiti,' said Herring.

'We're already fucking there! We just can't get ashore. I've been looking forward to fucking one of those Tahitian girls.'

'We all have, mate, but you've seen how hard it is against the wind. No matter what he tries we can't make headway.'

'I'm fucking exhausted. I reckon we would have been better off on Sarah Island,' said Irvine.

'You've got to be joking, mate,' said Herring.

The bell rang, signalling the end to the lunch break and all the men reluctantly went back to their posts.

All afternoon Captain Swallow tried to get the brig into the bay. At the end of the day, he mustered the crew in front of the poop deck.

Poop Deck *Cyprus*

'You can all see the position we are in, men. As you are aware we are in sight of Tahiti, but unless the wind drops we will not meet our objective. We are in desperate need to replenish our water supplies, as the water we have

56

left is putrid. The other issue and the most dangerous is there could well be a warship waiting to apprehend us.'

'Are there any other islands we could go to, captain?' asked several of the men.

'Aye, we could sail to the Friendly Isles also known as the Tongan Islands.'

'How far away are they?'

'Twelve hundred miles westward and if this breeze holds, which I believe it will, we could run before it with very little work. I estimate we could be there in a week.'

'I've heard the women on the Friendly Isles are just as beautiful and just as friendly as the women on Tahiti,' said Jones.

The rest of the crew laughed and hollered.

'It's off to the Friendly Isles we go.'

'We need to take a vote. All those in favour of changing our course for the Friendly Isles, raise your hand.'

The vote was unanimous.

The brig became a hive of harmonious activity, with each sailor doing his allocated task without complaint.

That changed when a few disgruntled crewmembers approached Captain Swallow.

'Captain, we're worried that you are taking us too close to New South Wales which is the last fucking place we want to be. We insist you change your course for Japan.'

'You men have no fucking idea how far Japan is. Our water situation is critical; we'd never make it halfway there. Not only that, the ship would have to pass through Equatorial Calms to reach the Northern Hemisphere. It could take up to two months to get to Japan.'

The mutinous group dispersed but remained a menacing presence until on the sixth day when they all heard the shout, "Land ho".

As Captain Swallow brought the brig closer into shore, they could see a high volcanic island covered in thick jungle which was girt by pristine white sand beaches where coconut palms lined the shore.

This island was known as Niue Island; Tasman had visited it in 1643 and Captain Cook in 1774.

Swallow shortened the sails and edged his way into the bay where it would seem the main village of the island was located. Native huts lined the beach and canoes lay waiting on the sand. He ordered the anchor to be dropped half a mile from the beach.

Canoes and outriggers with grass mat sails converged on *Cyprus* aka *Friends of Boston*. They were paddled by men. Women, all bare-breasted, sat or stood in the vessels madly waving at the crew.

It soon became obvious how the Friendly Isles got their name. A large outrigger stood out from the other vessels. An elderly distinguished- looking man wearing a cloak of feathers was sitting in the rear. The men discovered he was the King of Niue.

Swallow noticed a white man in the king's canoe who was dressed as a native. He sang out, 'What is your intention? Do you wish to trade?'

' We are *Friends of Boston* bound for China. We require fresh water, coconuts, pigs, breadfruit and any other fresh food you can supply. Who are you?'

'Joe Geeves. I am the king's interpreter.

'Come on board, Joe, and bring the king with you.'

'Do you have plenty of grog?'

'We do, plenty.'

'Excellent, so welcome *Friends of Boston* welcome to Niue Island where you will enjoy your stay, I can assure you.

Once Joe and the king were on board when a toast was made to friendship.

'Joe, how did you end up living here; an American on a south sea island?' asked Captain Swallow.

'Let's just say I left my ship without permission.'

Paradise Found

Chapter 12

For six magnificent weeks, *Friends* laid at anchor off Niue Island. No crewmember wished to leave this haven, which provided good food, sunshine and plenty of sex.

Initially, the Tongans both male and female were permitted to board the brig, and as a result, *Friends* became a vessel of grog and unabandoned sex. Captain Swallow had lost all control of the ship's crew and to a certain extent of the ship itself.

The day was filled with feasting, drinking singing, dancing and orgies.

'What do you reckon, Frank? Are these women any good or not? It's been years since I fucked a woman and today I've had three,' said Will.

'Have you? Bloody hell, I better catch up. I've only had two.'

After years of tyranny, floggings and being worked so hard they nearly died the escaped convicts knew they were in paradise.

'So Captain, now you can understand why I stayed here all this time? I get all the sex I can handle. I eat well and don't answer to anyone apart from the king, here,' said Joe.

'Yes, I can understand your reluctance to return to America.'

'The king has asked me to negotiate some gifts in return for our hospitality.'

'What do you exactly mean— negotiate?'

'Well, what I mean is you gift us things we require.'

'I see, and what do you require?'

'We'd like some blankets and leather.'

'Yes, we can provide you with those. Anything else?'

'There is, as a matter of fact. We'd like tobacco and grog for our enjoyment.'

'I'll see what I can do.'

'Thank you, Captain, much appreciated.'

'May I ask you how the brig was named *"Friends of Boston"* when it's obvious she's not an American ship? I was at sea for many years predominately on American whalers, so I know an American brig when I see one.'

'Let me ask you something before I answer your question, Joe. How come you are here and how did you get here?'

'I jumped ship when the whaler I was on stopped here for fresh water and provisions. I never did like civilisation much so I ran into the jungle and only returned when I saw my ship had sailed. I've been here for many years and have no intention of leaving. I speak the native language fluently and have six wives and so many children that I have trouble remembering all their names. So, what's your story, Captain?'

Captain Swallow recounted the entire story of how *Cyprus* was captured and renamed, and how they got to Tonga.

'Well that's quite a tale, Captain. You've all been through hell, so no wonder you are making hay while you are here.'

At dusk, all the villages departed back to their village. The king, through his interpreter Joe, invited the entire ship's crew to their village the following night for a feast.

Swallow and his two trusted first and second mates declined the invitation on the basis that somebody needed to keep watch on the ship.

The remainder of the crew rowed over to the village, knowing they were in for a night of feasting and lovemaking.

'Captain Swallow, there seem to be a lot of things missing from the ship,' said Arthur Templeton.

'What do you mean?'

'I went into the galley and noticed a significant amount of cutlery was missing, pots and pans too.'

'All right, we need to do a complete check to see what else has been stolen.'

The three men found that anything metallic that was accessible had been stolen. Knives, marine spikes etc. were gone. Also, items such as halyards, rolls of twine, blocks and tackles and two buckets had been taken.

Swallow knew all these items could be replaced by the brig's store, but nevertheless, he was furious.

He laid down the law.

'You may or may not know the natives have stolen a considerable amount of the ship's property while on board. There will be no more native visitors allowed on board apart from the king and Joe. The rule is only half the crew will be permitted to visit the village at any one time. The remaining half will be responsible for watching over the ship.'

'That seems a bit harsh, Captain. I hope the men accept the new rules.'

'Ferguson, they don't have a choice. Right, muster the crew to the front of the poop so I can explain the situation.'

It was dawn; and most of the crew were wiping the sleep from their eyes.

Captain Swallow explained the situation of the stolen property and the new rules as a result.

'Surely a few odds and sods won't make a difference, Captain. We're enjoying ourselves for the first time in years so let us have our fun,' said Thacker.

'You'll still have your fun, Thacker. You'll go ashore every second day and satisfy your appetites. Let me make it clear to you all; the reason for the new regime is to ensure the brig is kept in tiptop order. There is no doubt about it with the British Navy looking for us that we will have to leave this place. The brig is our only way of ensuring we don't stand on the gallows at Execution Dock.

'There's work we need to do such as cleaning the water tanks and bringing on clean fresh water, which will need to be replenished regularly.

'In other words, the brig needs to be kept in sailing trim.'

Captain Swallow's speech was met with scowls and disgruntled looks. Swallow was fearful of another mutiny.

However, the mates showed their support for the captain, ensuring the crew did not revolt.

'I hope it is clear to you all that only nine men go ashore on twenty-four hours leave. The remainder of you men stay on board until the first group returns,' shouted Ferguson.

No sooner had Ferguson shouted his command than several native canoes paddled up beside the brig. The crew had to fend them off and they soon got the idea. Nine of the crew returned to the village in the canoes bearing tobacco, grog, blankets and other trade goods.

The crew remaining on board looked on in envy, but they knew it would be their turn on the morrow.

As night drew those on board could hear the drums and song and laughter emanating from the village.

Later in the day, Joe Geeves paddled out to the brig in a small canoe. Once on board he was invited to sit down on the deck and the pirates gathered around him.

'Your shipmates are having a grand old time on shore and I believe it's your turn tomorrow. You've got something to look forward to. The king has ordered a feast for you all. Not only that, but he has ordered a wife for each of you to enjoy during your stay.'

The sailors looked at each other, grinning in anticipation.

'Joe, how long have you been living among the natives?' asked Jones.

'To be honest I'm not really sure. You lose track of time here.'

'Do you get many ships calling in?' asked Swallow.

'No, we're off the main sailing routes, but we do get the odd whaler like the one I was on. They'll trade for fresh water, pigs or coconuts but not very often. Most of them head for the big island of Tonga Taboo, about two hundred-and-fifty miles west of here.'

'How many islands comprise Tonga, Joe?'

'There's about a hundred-and-fifty. Some are inhabited, but some are just coral cays.'

'Does Tonga do much trade with the Europeans and Americans?' asked Ferguson.

'No, not really. All we have to trade is coconuts and nobody wants to buy them.'

'So no trade whatsoever?'

'The only trade we get is when a whaler or sealer calls in for water, pigs, taro or bananas. The other commodity they're interested in is our women.'

'So whalers and sealers are the only vessels that call in into Niue?'

'British warships come occasionally looking for escaped convicts. Some of the old men on the island still remember the *Bounty*. There's some similarity to you lot and the *Bounty* so let's hope it takes twenty years or more to find you as it did them.'

'I hope so; twenty years of freedom would do me. The problem we've got is there's a lot more shipping sailing the Pacific than in the time of the *Bounty*,' said Swallow.

'I think you're right, Captain; not many places to hide these days.'

'I hate to think about it but I'm afraid we'll have to scuttle the old girl one day soon.'

'Any idea where you'd like to settle?'

'We took a vote a while ago and the consensus was America.'

'How in the fuck would you get to America?'

'We were thinking a whaler would take us there.'

'There's no way a whaler would take on eighteen men off a brig in the middle of the ocean. He might take a few from an island but not all of you.'

The next morning Swallow called Ferguson into his cabin.

'Ferguson, as you know it's been six weeks since we arrived at Niue. The break has been good for the men, very good, but I think it's time we sailed again. I keep thinking we will see a warship enter the bay at any time.'

'I tend to agree with you, Captain, as much as I regret leaving this place. Have you thought about where we might go?'

'There are a few options. Japan or China would be on the top of my list. Although the Pacific is desirable, the shipping traffic is becoming quite intense. The odds of being apprehended are quite strong. If we head for the northern hemisphere we are more likely to remain anonymous. We may also have a better chance of retuning to England,' said Swallow.

'Fair enough. Would you like me to muster the men so we can take a vote?'

'Yes, that would be good, thanks, Ferguson.'

The crew assembled in front of the poop deck the following day at 8 am. The shift that missed their visit to the island was extremely disgruntled.

Captain Swallow made the announcement regarding raising the anchor and moving on.

'The longer we stay the higher the chance of being apprehended. If we were captured the chances are we would all be hanged for piracy.'

'So where do you reckon we should go, Captain?' asked Reynolds.

'That's a good question. My suggestion is Japan or China.'

'Why don't we take the brig out to deep water and scuttle her? Then we can live the remainder of our days shagging women and be eating like kings,' said Smythe.

'I understand your feelings but after a while, I'm sure you all will yearn for some civilisation. If we sail to China, for instance, we could scuttle the ship off her coast and pretend we were shipwrecked. That way we could sail back to England as free men.'

'Well, I for one aren't going anywhere. I'm staying here with my wife,' said

Briant.

'I'm with you, Briant. I'm staying put. Fuck China and Japan,' said Towers.

'All right, we'll take a vote,' said Captain Swallow.

A vote was taken and seven convicts voted to stay on the island.

The remainder of the crew would sail to Japan and China with Captain Swallow. Ferguson wasn't one of them.

I Think I'm Turning Japanese

I Really Think So

Chapter 13

'Ferguson I think it's time we got the men together for a meeting on board,' said Captain Swallow.

'Aye Captain… to discuss what, exactly?'

'A decision needs to be made as to who's staying and who's coming with me to Japan.'

' Seeing they're all having such a good time with their wives I'm not sure how many will elect to leave this paradise.'

'That's what we need to find out. If we don't have a crew, none of us will be going anywhere. We can just stay here until a British warship finds us.'

'I'll call the men together, Captain. Exactly when do you want the meeting?'

'Let's make it 10 am tomorrow. That will give those on shore time to get back to the ship.'

'Yes, sir.'

Cyprus **Poop Deck**

When 10 am had ticked over Ferguson called the meeting to order.

'Listen up, men; the Captain wants to say a few words.'

Swallow stepped forwards. 'As you all know, we have been anchored off Niue for several weeks. It's been a wonderful break for us all but now the time has come to decide who's staying and who's sailing to Japan. For those who decide to stay, be aware of the danger of a warship finding you. You will all hang. The option to sail to Japan is a safer one as the British have very little presence in the area.

'All those who wish to stay put your hand up.'

Leslie Ferguson, Paddy Lynch, Tom Campbell, George Gates, Harry

Briant, Charles Towers and Bill Templeton all raised their hands. Swallow was surprised Ferguson had elected to stay.

November 15

The brig, newly provisioned with food and fresh water, raised her sails and sailed out of Niue Bay leaving the five comrades and a number of grieving wives behind. The eleven remaining crew members would have their work cut out for them.

Destination Japan.

Swallow appointed George Davis as first mate. He and Jones were the only men among the remaining ten who had any sailing experience. The others had learned the ropes while sailing from Tasmania but were slow to react to tricky situations when they occurred.

The brig proceeded westerly across the Pacific Ocean, passing by many tropical islands including Samoa, the Ellice Islands, the Gilbert Islands and the Marshall Islands.

The first and second mate were no longer present as they had elected to stay on Niue, and with that came a lack of discipline on the brig. The remaining eleven had only one desire; to go back home to England or at worse case, America. They yearned to live in a civilised society.

Captain Swallow knew the only way of maintaining discipline on the brig was fear. He emphasised the chances of encountering a hurricane or being wrecked on a reef was high. He also made it known that the British Navy had a high presence in the Pacific.

The only person that could steer them through these hazards was William Swallow.

Swallow was very cautious. If the wind became fresh, he shortened the sail at night or if they encountered a storm he would "heave to", bringing the ship to a virtual standstill. Although his methods ensured painful progress, it was safe. His lack of a full crew made it necessary to adopt this strategy.

The luxury items such as cheese, butter, tobacco and grog were becoming very low. In abundance was pickled pork, salt beef and biscuits, but the crew were becoming restless.

The crew were becoming disobedient, ignoring orders and refusing to haul the sails. There were constant quarrels, which in some cases resulted in fights. The decks were allowed to become filthy, as were the men's living quarters. Sails that need repair were ignored.

Captain Swallow was at his wit's end.

The ship was navigating through the Marshall Islands. There are twenty-four inhabited islands and another ten uninhabited.

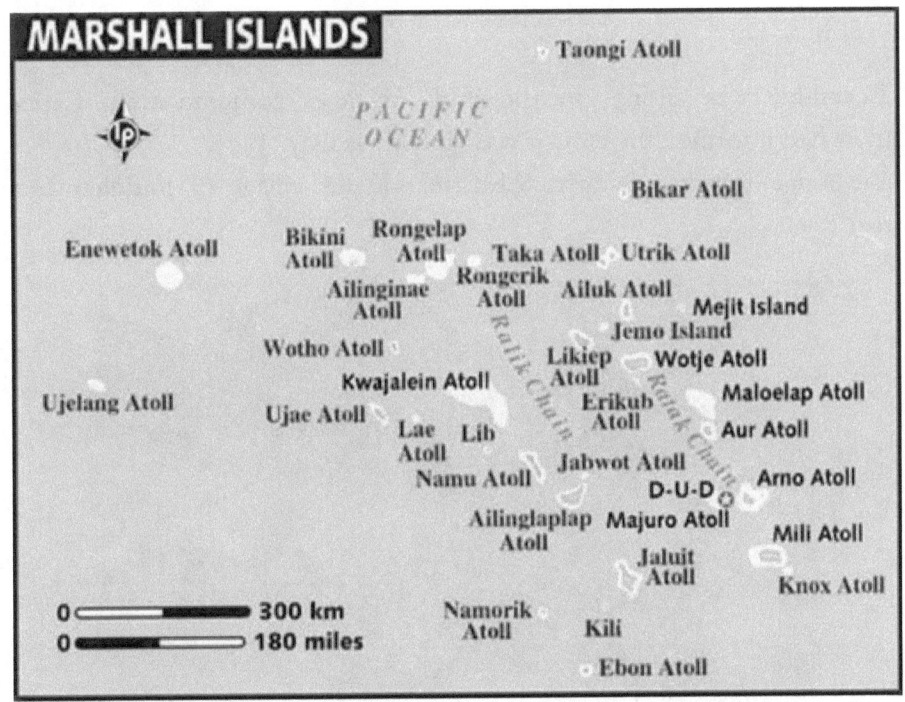

Captain Swallow decide to restock with wood and fresh water and he chose a large atoll, Majoro. The island provided shelter for the ship and the natives seemed to be friendly.

'Men, we are anchored here until we can be restocked with wood and water so we can continue on to Japan. This is not a pleasure stop like Niue. Only four men will be permitted ashore at once,' said Captain Swallow.

'Why don't we just scuttle the fucking ship and live with the natives? We might be lucky enough to be picked up by a whaler and get to America,' said Davis.

'I'm with you, Davis. I'm sick of this stinking ship.'

'We'll take a vote, but let me make it clear; it must be a unanimous result either way. If it's a split decision I decide.'

The vote was taken and the tally was four to stay and seven to sail to Japan.

Swallow knew he would need to watch out for a mutiny.

Ten days later with the water tanks full, *Friends* sailed off, heading due east.

Christmas Day 1829

Beveridge was sitting on the deck in quiet contemplation. Captain Swallow had informed the crew it was Christmas Day.

Beveridge reflected back to Christmas in his village of Puddletown in Dorset.

He thought about the Christmas Days he spent with his family, his mother and father and two sisters. Snow would be covering all in the village, turning it into a winter wonderland.

His mother would cook turkey and plum pudding. His father would skilfully carve the bird. The day was filled with laughter and frivolity.

Now he was dressed in filthy rags; a fugitive that, if apprehended, would more than likely hang. His Christmas lunch would be pickled pork like every other fucking day.

Beveridge was not alone in his melancholy. The other crewmembers were in a similar space.

Christmas was a day of sadness.

Three days after Christmas, the *Friends* was almost ready to leave the Marshall Islands and head for Japan, a land of mystery.

Watts was checking the sails from the bosun's chair aloft when he saw something from the corner of his eye; it was a three-masted schooner flying an American flag.

'Ship ahoy to the starboard side.'

The entire crew raced to the starboard side to observe the schooner approaching the atoll. She sailed into the bay and anchored.

She was a Nantucket whaler and she lowered her longboat and rowed over to the *Friends*.

Once the boat was close enough to communicate the first mate yelled out, 'what brig is that?'

'*Friends of Boston* bound for China,' responded Captain Swallow.

'I can't say I've heard of you. Who are your owners?'

'Darling Brothers.'

'I know Boston like the back of me fucking hand. There are no Darling Brothers in Boston. If you're pirates be prepared to meet thy maker.'

Swallow looked over at the schooner and noted the whaler had gunports down the side of her lower deck.

'I assure you, sir, we are not pirates.'

'Then who are you?'

'I have to be truthful. We are convicts who escaped the tyranny of the New South Wales cruel penal system.'

'What is your intention?'

'Sir, if you took us on board your ship we would scuttle the brig. We are all keen to live in America.'

'How many of you are there?'

'Eleven, sir.'

'That's a small crew for that size brig. I'll consult the captain to see if we can accommodate you all.'

The longboat returned to the schooner. It was a pensive wait for the crew. The first mate returned in the boat, pulling up alongside the brig's rope ladder. He boarded the ship and addressed Captain Swallow.

'Bad news I'm afraid we don't have room for you and your crew and besides, we are at the beginning of our hunt and we won't be returning to

Nantucket for at least a year. The Captain wishes to know if you have sufficient provisions for your journey to China.'

'Yes, we have ample; in fact you may wish to purchase some from us.'

'What have you got for sale?'

'We can sell you pickled pork, four barrels in all, along with four barrels of biscuits. We can also sell you twenty blankets, an unused coil of rope and a sizeable piece of leather.'

'How much are you asking, Captain?'

'One hundred silver dollars.'

'Can you let me see the goods?'

'Certainly, my first mate will show you.'

The two men returned to Swallow having inspected the goods.

'They all look good quality to me I'll ask the captain if he wishes to purchase them.'

The whaler returned to the *Friends* with 100 silver dollars in a bag; the deal was done. Captain Swallow was delighted as he knew they would need this money in Japan and possibly China.

Swallow gave each man five silver dollars. The balance would remain in Captain Swallow's cabin.

'Well, men that was a stroke of luck! We'll heave up the anchor and sail at once.'

As the Americans were about to cast off, one of *Friends'* crew, John Denner, tried to join them. Two crewmen seized him and threw him onto the deck.

'Where do you think you're going, you cowardly bastard?'

'I just want to go to America.'

'And leave us a crewman short.'

Captain Swallow intervened. 'Put him in irons. That will stop the coward from deserting ship.'

The men looked at each other in shock. All those years being fettered in irons and now one of their own would suffer that fate once again.

Bob McGuire, who replaced Ferguson as Master-at-Arms, stepped forward.

'Obey your captain. He's right. Anyone who attempts to desert should be put in irons.'

Bob went down to his cabin to fetch a pair of fetters. He had only two pairs as most had been thrown overboard when they seized the ship.

Returning, he riveted a pair of leg irons to the sobbing Denner. Some of the crewmembers scowled while others were approving.

The next task for the crew was to heave up the anchor, shake out the foresail and topsails, and set the jibs. They were sailing to Japan.

With Captain Swallow at the wheel, the *Friends* sailed out of the bay. As she passed the American schooner her crew waved and wished the motley crew good luck.

Captain Swallow found the navigation through the myriad of islands difficult, for there were submerged rocks and coral reefs to contend with. Finally the brig found open seas.

Swallow set a course north by west, which would take them to their destination. He hoped, as they all did, that Japan would be the haven they all sought.

Reflecting back on the five months it had been since sailing out of Recherche Bay, Swallow couldn't help feeling proud of his achievements. He had never captained a ship before nor navigated a vessel over such long distances.

The crew began to see strange sailing craft in the distance. They turned out to be Japanese fishing boats.

'The coast of Japan must be near,' said George Davis to no one in particular.

Captain Swallow hoped they would be able to perform some maintenance on the brig while in Japan; her sails were in much need of repairing and some ropes needed replacing. They were also very low on fresh water and wood.

What Swallow didn't know was Japan was a closed country. The only foreigners permitted to trade were the Dutch and they were restricted to one port, Nagasaki.

The Japanese Emperor had ruled that no Japanese citizen was to trade or communicate with foreigners apart from in Nagasaki.

The fishing boats they first sighted were all sailing away from the brig at good speed and they had no chance to contact them. The crew couldn't understand why.

None of the charts Captain Swallow had access to covered Japan so he would have to take his chances in finding a port.

He sailed southwards, hugging the coastline and looking for a safe haven.

On January 22 the brig sighted a reasonably large town with many fishing boats anchored in the harbour. The town was Shimoda, which serviced the city of Yokohama. He waited for a pilot boat to escort the brig into harbour but none came.

Swallow was concerned. He could not see any Dutch ships at anchor in the harbour, but he noted a fortress on a hill with canon pointing directly at the brig.

He then noticed a boat heading for them. Apart from the oarsmen, it contained soldiers and an officer in an elaborate uniform.

The soldiers and the officer climbed on board. Swallow could see this official was disgusted with the state of Cyprus's deck and sails. The state of the crew didn't impress him either.

The officer started to address Swallow in Japanese but the English pirate made it known he did not speak Japanese. Swallow used sign language to communicate their need for wood and fresh water.

The officer used sign language to tell Swallow his request needed to be in writing. Swallow responded by writing out a note, which the officer took with him back to the town.

Four hours later the officer and his entourage returned to the brig. He pointed to the open sea, indicating strongly that the brig was not welcome to stay and must leave immediately.

He pointed to the sun, indicating the ship must sail by sunset.

Finally, he pointed to the fort with its canon indicating that if he disobeyed his command they would blast the brig out of the water.

The Japanese then departed. The crew and Captain Swallow were mystified and horrified at the lack of hospitality; any other port in the world would have welcomed them.

What the crew of the Cyprus didn't know was the local shogun who had made the decision was under strict instruction not to aid or communicate with foreigners, as was the whole of Japan. If he had agreed to Swallow's request he would have lost his life.

The above Japanese print was discovered recently it is believed to be the Cyprus brig.

CHINA

CHAPTER 14

After the Japanese official had disembarked, Captain Swallow called a meeting.

'Well, men, it's obvious we are not welcome in Japan for whatever reason. That begs the question where to now? My suggestion would be China.'

A vote was taken and the majority voted for China.

'Right, China it is. We'll need to wait for the wind to pick up before we get underway.'

When the sun had set for the day, the Japanese ultimatum came into force.

The canons of the fort fired their first volley, landing just short of the brig. These shots were meant as a warning.

'Holy fuck, they're firing on us. Come on let's get out of here,' said George Davis.

Captain Swallow ordered the sails to be set and raised the anchor. Those actions achieved nothing as they were becalmed in the bay.

Their Japanese hosts were not satisfied with the progress being made; they fired another cannon ball directly at the *Friends,* ripping through the lower stern of the ship.

Fortuitously a slight breeze sprung up allowing the *Friends* to slowly move out of the harbour, all the while being peppered by Japanese canon.

Captain Swallow was yet to inspect the damage below as he had been too preoccupied in sailing out of range of the Japanese fortress. He was thankful that the breeze was still light, allowing the brig to sail at an easy three knots.

Swallow ordered one of the crew to take the wheel while he went astern to determine the damage. As he climbed down the steps, he found eight inches of water covering the lower deck. He immediately climbed up to the top deck and ordered all crew to man the pumps. Despite their weariness, they had no other option.

Captain Swallow's ordered his two mates, first and second, to go below and endeavour to plug the leak. This they did with canvas, hemp and pitch

74

and they then hammered planks into the hull to secure it all.

Once Captain Swallow was convinced the brig was seaworthy, he set a course for the Mariana Islands hoping they could replenish their water and wood. A shallow berth would also enable them to perform repairs where the cannon ball entered the ship.

The going was very slow and Captain Swallow was very aware of the brig's vulnerability. After a week's sailing they sighted what they thought was Thieves Islands, so named by the Portuguese navigator Magellan in 1521. The crew thought the name ironic, but soon discovered an error.

Whether it be through exhaustion or incorrect readings, they had stumbled upon the Nansei Archipelago, a Chinese protectorate, instead.

Swallow sailed into a bay on one of the larger islands where they could see activity. There they were able to trade blankets for fresh water and a supply of wood.

Captain Swallow could sense the mood of discontent among the crew and knew a mutiny was more than possible. He decided to call a meeting so at least they could all have a say about what they should do next.

'I'm for scuttling the brig here right now and taking our chances on the island. You never know— we might get picked up by a whaler,' said Herring

'I'm with you, Herring. We've been on this brig long enough and it's time to settle on dry land,' said Watts.

'I have no problem in scuttling the brig, but I suggest we should do so near Canton; we'll have a better chance of passage back to England,' said Captain Swallow.

'I want to get off this ship now anyway. The longboat won't take ten of us when she's scuttled in the South China Sea. Give me some provisions, row me assure, and I won't be any more trouble to you all,' said John Denner.

The other crewmembers listened to Denner's plea. He was the bastard who'd tried to abscond in the Marshal Islands. If caught, he'd say he was forced to join the crew and the marks on his ankles would lay testament to his claim.

'Do you think we should put him in irons again and throw him overboard?' said Thacker.

'Listen, none of us aboard are serving a sentence for murder, so let's keep it that way,' said Swallow.

The rest of the crew agreed with their captain.

'I'll go with Denner to keep him company,' said Pennell.

'Bloody hell mate, they're taking a risk, hoping the Chinese will take them in. They don't speak the language and know nothing about the Chinese culture,' said Jones.

'I agree— better them than me. I'd rather take my chances in Canton,' said Davis.

Captain Swallow gave each man ten silver dollars. They were then put into the longboat along with a cask of pickled pork, a barrel of biscuits a dozen blankets and a jar of rum for the first night.

Jones called out 'good luck,' as they rowed back to the brig. The two men looked pensive as they waved the ship goodbye.

Captain Swallow called the crew together.

'Right, men we need to have our story straight. We can no longer call ourselves *Friends of Boston* as it is obvious we are not American. The authorities would pick us out in an instant by our English accents. From here on we are *Edward of London*, and the captain of said ship is Waldron, not Swallow.'

'Won't they know we are *Friends* by the name painted on the bow?' asked the youngest member of the crew, George Davis.

'George we are scuttling the brig in deep water so they will never know. Now remember *Edward* and Waldron. Don't forget it as I know some of you are prone to forget. We departed England from the port of Blackwall twelve months ago and we got shipwrecked off the coast of Formosa.

'If they ask you any more questions feign ignorance or claim you forgot. Most of you should have no trouble pulling that one off.

'Right, set the sails and raise the anchor—we head for Canton.'

Even though the sails were tattered and torn the *Cyprus* aka *Friends* aka *Edward* could still catch the breeze.

As the brig sailed towards Canton at five knots, Captain Waldron aka Swallow reflected on the past six months. He knew they were sailing into the clutches of British Justice; a system he knew well. They would either convince the authorities of their shipwreck story or they would all be hanged but either way they had all had their fling. It had to be better than six months on Sarah Island.

CHINESE PIRATES

CHAPTER 15

It was six months to the day since the *Cyprus* sailed out of Recherche Bay and she had now rounded Formosa heading for the busy port of Canton.

Sailing in the South China Sea had its dangers; Chinese pirates were very active in these waters. The most feared pirate Lord was Ching Shih.

Ching Shih was a beautiful Chinese woman who by necessity chose to be a prostitute. From these humble beginnings, she went on to control the largest pirate fleet the world has ever known, the Red Flag Fleet.

One of her clients was the pirate Zhèng Yi. It was he that established the Red Flag Fleet with 200 pirate ships under his command. Zhèng Yi was under Ching Shih's spell. He asked her to marry him and she accepted only on the basis she would own 50% of the Red Flag Fleet. Zhèng Yi knew she was smart. He also she was shrewd. She would be an asset to him in growing his empire.

The married couple grew the fleet to 600 ships in a short space of time. On Ching Shih's suggestion, they formed the Cantonese Pirate Coalition with a rival pirate Wu Shi'er. Zhèng. This coalition proved to be extremely successful but unfortunately her husband died during a journey to Vietnam just six years after the marriage. Ching Shih took over the fleet consisting of 600 ships and 20,000 pirates. She proved to be a formable leader, signing additional agreements with rival pirates. She established a partnership with her stepson Cheung Po who also became her lover.

Red Flag Junk

The pirate queen knew with such a large band of pirates under her control a set of rules needed to be drafted and strictly enforced.

1. Anyone giving their own orders (ones that did not come down from Ching Shih) or disobeying those of a superior, was beheaded on the spot.
2. No one was to steal from the public fund or any villagers that supplied the pirates.
3. All goods taken as booty had to be presented for group inspection. The booty was registered by a purser and then distributed by the

fleet leader. The original seizer received twenty percent and the rest was placed into the public fund.

4. Actual money was turned over to the squadron leader, who gave a small amount back to the seizer, so the rest could be used to purchase supplies for unsuccessful ships. The punishment for a first-time offence of withholding booty was severe whipping of the back. Large amounts of withheld treasure or subsequent offences carried the death penalty.

Ching Shih's code had special rules for female captives.

Usually, the pirates made their most beautiful captives their concubines or wives. If a pirate took a wife he had to be faithful to her. The ones deemed unattractive were released and any remaining were ransomed. Pirates that raped female captives were put to death. If pirates had consensual sex with captives, the pirate was beheaded and the woman had cannonballs attached to her legs and was thrown over the side of the boat.

They were tough rules for a very tough business.

The pirate queen continued to grow her fleet and at the peak of her rule she commanded over 1500 ships and 50,000 pirates.

After years of waging war with the Chinese Government and rival pirate fleets, she decided to retire. She requested special dispensation to marry her stepson Cheung Po which was given by the Governor of Guangdong.

She moved back to Guangzhou and opened a gambling house and a brothel.

DECEPTION

CHAPTER 16

Captain Swallow was pleased with the progress they were making and he estimated they would be off Canton the following day. His intention was to scuttle the ship and transfer to the longboat before sailing to Canton then telling their tale of being shipwrecked off Formosa. The crew could see fishing junks on the horizon going about their business. One junk stood out because it was almost as large as the brig yet its speed was quite astounding. It must have been doing ten knots. It didn't take long for this vessel to be aside the brig. All the crew were observing from the main deck, not knowing what was going on.

Next thing, a grappling hook caught the rail and then another and another. They were being attacked by Chinese pirates. These pirates were no ordinary pirates; they belonged to the Red Flag Fleet.

There were twenty pirates on board in a very short time and Captain Swallow shouted out to the crew not to fight back.

The pirates indicated to the crew to assemble in front of the poop deck and sit down with their hands in front of them.

The last pirate on board was obviously the captain. He spoke no English and Swallow knew no Chinese so they both reverted to hand signals.

Captain Swallow noticed the captain looking around the deck, which was filthy. He looked up at the sails and observed their terrible condition. At this point, he obviously realised he was wasting his time.

He ordered his men to leave the ship. There was other quarry they could pursue.

Swallow was thankful they didn't find the silver dollars he had hidden under a floorboard in his cabin.

The *Edward* sailed into the South China Sea, heading for the port city of Canton.

They all kept their eyes peeled for British warships protecting the trading ships of the East Indian Trading Company. They were always present in and around Canton.

Captain Swallow knew it was time to scuttle the *Cyprus* aka *Edward of*

London. He had planned it from the outset, but now that it was time he felt sorry he had to sink her in such an undignified way. She had done them proud and without her they would be labouring as slaves on Sarah Island.

Just as the crew were about to scuttle her hull, a fishing junk pulled alongside of the ship. To their surprise, the Chinaman in charge yelled out to them in English.

'Are you an English ship?'

' Yes, we are. Where are you from?' yelled Captain Swallow.

'Whampoa.'

'Is that close to Canton?'

'Yes, it is in the mouth of the Canton River.'

'Where did you learn to speak English?'

'Many British and Dutch ships anchor there.'

Four of the crew approached their captain.

'Captain, we would like to sail into Canton on the junk,' said Davis, Jones, Herring and Stevenson.

'Why would you want to do that?

'We don't feel comfortable sailing in on the longboat even though she now has *Edward* painted on her sides. We'd feel safer if we went with the junk.'

'Well, you better strike a deal with the captain before you commit.'

Davis negotiated a fare of eight silver dollars per man. All four fugitives boarded the junk and they were on their way. Now there were four to sail the longboat into Canton Harbour.

First, they needed to put a hole in the hull big enough for it to sink quickly.

Swallow ordered two of his remaining crew to follow him down into the bowels of the ship. Swallow gathered a bag of carpenter's tools. He then cut away the sealing on the bottom of the brig and removed two of the planks and copper sheathing. Water gushed through the hole as the three men took their exit.

They lowered the longboat, still tethered to the brig, down into the choppy sea. They had stocked her with their sea bags, as well as oars, a mast, a sail, a barrel of drinking water, some salted beef and biscuits, muskets, ammunition, compass, quadrant, telescope and various other items of value. The last item was Swallow's fake ship's log.

Captain Swallow remained on deck to ensure the ship was heading for Canton albeit at a very slow rate of knots. When she was so low in the water as to become dangerous, he joined his men in the boat.

Captain Swallow aka Waldron navigated the boat towards the Canton River. He was contemplating his fate and the story they would all tell the British authorities upon arrival in Canton. He decided the log he faked would be more detrimental than helpful, so he ditched it over the side.

It took a day's sailing to reach Lin Tin Island, about forty-five miles from Whampoa Reach in the Canton River. A junk sailed close to the longboat and when another Chinese man hailed them in English, the four men were astounded.

'Hello, Englishmen, what are you doing in such a small boat?'

'We were shipwrecked off the Formosan coast and we are attempting to get to Canton.'

'You are not far. Maybe a day's sailing.'

'Are you aware if there any British or foreign ships in Canton Harbour?'

'Yes, there are several British merchant ships and a Danish ship.'

'So there are no British warships?'

'No, not that I'm aware.'

'May I ask where you learned such good English?'

'I was a steward on an East Indian merchant ship. I have made many voyages to London.'

'Thank you. We wish you well, sir.'

'I wish you well. Take care in that boat.'

'Just before you go, Captain, seeing you're a pilot would it be possible to tether us and take us to Lin Tin Island?'

'Yes, I can do that, but I would have to charge you a small fee.'

'How much?'

'Four dollars.'

'Agreed.'

They were towed in and released at the wharf. Soon the eight pirates were together again.

'Men, we have to ensure we tell our story with conviction. If we convince the authorities we are victims of a shipwreck, then we will be on a ship back to England as free men.

'Remember, I'm Captain Waldron of the Edward of London, which hit a reef off Formosa. When we dock at Canton I will do the talking. If necessary, Jones and Stevenson as first and second mates will support me.

'The story we will be telling them is we were on our way to Manila after being denied the right to trade with the Japanese. The brig foundered on a reef in a fierce storm and the *Edward* sank with ten men aboard. All were lost but we eight survived.

'Right men, shall we go down to the wharf and get underway?'

'I'm not going, Captain. I'm staying here,' said George Davis.

'What do you mean, George? We're all in this together,' said Swallow.

'Not me. I'm going to stay with a Chinese family on the island. I'll try and get away myself later.'

'Suit yourself. Come on men, we need to get moving. The Chinaman is getting impatient.'

The junk operator towed them to Whampoa at the mouth of the Canton River.

Moored in the river was a ship of the East India Trading Company. The longboat pulled alongside and asked permission to come aboard. Permission was granted and the seven unkempt sailors climbed the rope ladder.

The ship was the *Charles Grant;* a magnificent vessel beautifully decked out; fast, yet sturdy. She was manned with an expert crew.

The captain of the ship greeted the shipwrecked crew of seven, survivors of a horrendous shipwreck where ten crewmen lost their lives.

He listened to Swallow's story and his plea for safe passage to London so he could report the loss of *Edward* to the brig's owners.

'The owners must be informed as soon as possible so they can lodge an insurance claim,' said Swallow.

'Who are the owners?'

'Isaac & Son of Blackwall.'

'I've never heard of them.'

'They only ever owned one ship and that was the *Edward*. Now that she's gone they need the insurance money to purchase another brig.'

'May I peruse the ship's log?'

'I'm afraid you can't. When I went to my cabin to retrieve all the ship's papers, including the log, my cabin was full of water. I was lucky to make it to the longboat before she sank.'

'Are you looking for passage back to England as a passenger?'

'No sir, I am happy to work my way as an able seaman.'

'Good heavens, man, you were the master of a ship. I'll appoint you as a quartermaster. We have three other quartermasters on the ship and you can join them.'

'I appreciate your generosity, Captain. May I ask you to take on my crew? They are more than competent at the sail.'

'How many?'

'Six, sir, all good men.'

'I'm restricted to the number of crew I can take on, but I will take three. There are other ships in the harbour and I'm sure they will find passage with one of them.'

'Do you know where these ships are heading, sir?'

'The *Kellie Castle* is due to sail soon after us. She is bound for England. There is also a Dutch ship, the *Pulen*, due to sail soon although she's heading for New Orleans in America.'

'Thank you, Captain, I know of one or two who would like to go to America.'

'One more thing— you and your men must go into Canton tomorrow where the Committee of Supercargos will receive your depositions regarding the loss of your brig. They will provide you with Shipping Notes, to allow you and your men to be signed on as shipwrecked seamen.'

'Thank you very much, Captain, we all appreciate what you are doing.'

'Very well.'

'When do we sail, sir?'

'In five days' time, so make sure you return to the ship as soon as you have reported to the committee.'

'Yes, sir.'

'Right, well you and your men can bunk down on the ship.'

'Thank you, sir.'

Waldron aka Swallow took his men to the sleeping deck. Although cramped, it was a lot better than their quarters in the brig.

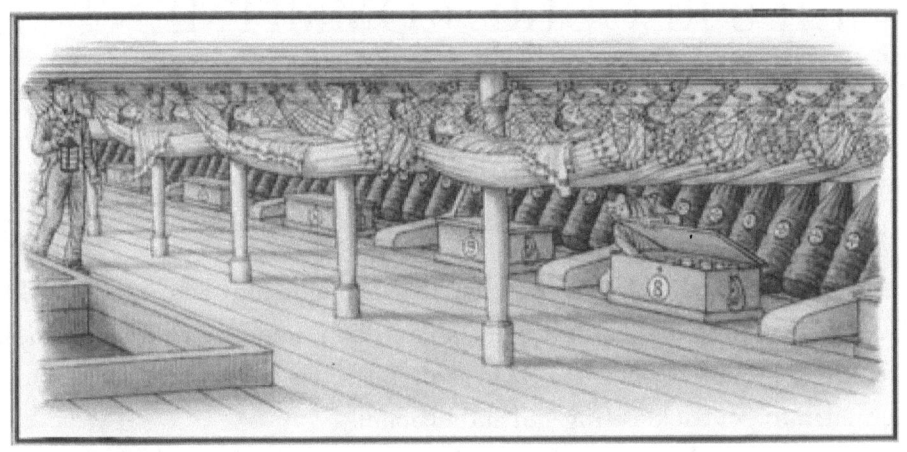

The following day, the group made their way into Canton primed to convince the committee of the truthfulness of their story. All went well. The remaining seamen of the shipwrecked brig *Edward* were issued Shipping Notes. As they returned to *Charles Grant,* they chuckled among themselves they had pulled the wool over the authorities' eyes.

March 5 1830

The *Charles Grant* and the *Pulen* weighed anchor and sailed together into the South China Seas, and once they cleared Lin Tin Island, they went their separate ways.

Quartermaster Waldron proved to the captain he was more than capable at the wheel.

LIES REQUIRE COMMITMENT

Veronica Roth, Divergent

CHAPTER 17

George Davis was hiding on the junk that brought him across to Lin Tin Island. He was frustrated at not being able to communicate with his Chinese hosts. Also, the loneliness of being on his own made him even more determined to get back to England and his family.

He paid the junkman two dollars to take him to the *Kellie Castle,* the sister ship of the *Charles Grant* which was anchored in Whampoa Reach.

Requesting to speak to the captain he asked if he could seek voyage back to England. He had changed his name to Huntley, a shipwrecked sailor from the brig, *Edward.*

The captain had heard about the fate of the *Edward* and was sympathetic to young Huntley's plight. He arranged for Huntley to be interviewed by the Committee of Supercargo so that he could receive his Shipping Notes, therefore allowing him to be a crewmember on the voyage back to England.

George was asked to sit in the waiting room. After about fifteen minutes, a distinguished looking man greeted the young seafarer, ushering him into the large meeting room.

Waiting were three more gentlemen all in their fifties. These men were all experienced merchants who owned trading vessels and they were also experienced mariners.

'Please, take a seat Mr Huntley. We have a few questions to ask you before we issue your Shipping Notes,' said Isaac Newman, the chairman of the committee.

'Could you please tell us in your own words the journey you undertook prior to being shipwrecked?'

'Yes, certainly; we began our voyage in Sydney, New South Wales. We sailed to New Zealand where we offloaded cargo and took on fresh provisions. We then sailed to Tahiti.'

'Excuse me for interrupting, Mr Huntley, but why was it that you sailed to Tahiti? It is hardly a trading port.'

'I'm not sure, sir; it was Captain Swallow's decision.'

'Who exactly is Captain Swallow?'

'Oh I apologise, he was my captain before Captain Waldron.'

'I see. Continue on, Mr Huntley.'

'We then sailed to Tonga where we traded and took on fresh water and wood.'

'Again, Mr Huntley, Tonga is not known for its trade.

'What other ships did you sail on prior to the *Edward*?'

'The *Edward* was the first ship I sailed on, sir.'

'Mr Huntley, the committee is not satisfied with the answers you have provided.

'You will sale to England on the *Kellie Castle* but as a prisoner, not as a free man. We suspect you of being involved in a mutiny or piracy or some other illegal activity, which will require further investigation.'

The captain of the *Kellie Castle* was informed of George's status and instructed to hand the prisoner over to the Thames Police for further investigation.

If he had informed on his comrades and told the real story, he may have been spared his fate. There was no doubt his fellow pirates would have informed on him to save their necks.

March 15 1830

The *Kellie Castle* weighed anchor and set sail for England. Ten days prior to this, the *Charles Grant* had set sail for the same destination.

Six months of sailing lay before them; twelve thousand miles in all.

Although it was not a race, the master of the *Kellie Castle* was keen to arrive in London before the *Charles Grant*, and with that in mind and the knowledge that her sister ship had departed before her, the captain set full sails and crowded on canvas. If the *Kellie Castle* did enter port first, justice could possibly be done.

Captain Finnegan decided to investigative Davis aka Huntley during the long voyage. He called upon one of his young crewmembers, Billy Armstrong, to help him.

'You called for me, Captain,' said Billy, with great trepidation.

'Yes Armstrong I have a job for you, a very important job.'

'Yes, sir.'

'You're aware I agreed to take on a shipwrecked sailor in Canton, no doubt. His name is George Huntley although I suspect that is not his real name.'

'Yes, sir, although I haven't met him yet.'

'Well, I want you to meet him and befriend him. I suspect he's either a mutineer or a pirate or both. Any information you can glean from him needs to be reported back to me. Do you understand?'

'Yes, sir, I will do my best.'

'Good. Now off you go. I will ensure you are always on the same shift as Huntley.'

'Thank you, Captain.'

That same day Billy found himself scrubbing the decks alongside George Huntley. Billy started up a conversation.

'Hello, my name is Billy Armstrong. What's yours?'

'George Huntley.'

'I'm pleased to meet you, George. Have you been sailing long?'

'No, not really. This is only my second ship. My first went down in a fierce storm off Formosa. I was lucky to survive.'

'Goodness me! I can't imagine what that would have been like.'

'We lost ten sailors; God rest their souls.'

'Oh my God, that's terrible.'

The first mate approached the two young men.

'That's enough lads, clean up and go down to wash before supper.'

'Yes, sir,' they responded together.

'Would it be all right if I sat next to you at supper?' asked Billy.

'Yes, certainly, Billy; you're the only crewmember I've spoken to.'

At supper, the two young men talked about their birthplaces in England. Billy came from Liverpool, while George was from Manchester. The two seamen became inseparable over the next month, and every now and again George would let slip with information the captain would like to hear.

When the *Kellie Castle* rounded the Cape of Good Hope, the ship's master gave the order for all crew to receive an extra tot of rum.

Billy and George were enjoying their extra rum when another crewmember offered the two friends his ration of rum. He said he didn't drink.

They accepted eagerly, and by the time they had drunk it all they were both feeling slightly drunk.

It was at this point in time that George confessed to Billy the true story of the *Cyprus* and how the convicts pirated the ship.

Billy felt sorry for George because he knew that once convicted on his evidence, George would be most likely hanged.

However, he had an obligation to report his findings to the captain.

The captain was most impressed with Billy, rewarding him with £5.

The captain did not inform George of the information Billy had passed on. He decided to hold onto it until he met with the Thames police when they reached port.

As far as George was concerned he was under suspicion no more.

AFRICA AND BEYOND

CHAPTER 18

May 28 1830

The four pirates under Swallow's control were well thought of on the *Charles Grant* as they behaved well and completed their work without complaint.

They had been at sea for two and a half months, and their next port of call was Cape Town in South Africa. William Swallow felt some trepidation as he was concerned that word had spread to Cape Town in regards to the seizing of the *Cyprus*. It was unlikely this would be the case as few ships sailed from Hobart Town or Sydney Town to Cape Town, but nevertheless he was nervous as the *Charles Grant* anchored in Table Bay.

Fresh water and wood were brought aboard the ship as well as fresh provisions. In addition, mail and newspapers from home were brought aboard.

None of the recipients of mail or newspapers made mention of the seizure of the *Cyprus,* much to Swallow's relief.

Table Bay 1830

Captain Everest set sail, still leading the *Kellie Castle* home although the sister ship was now only a few days behind and closing fast.

As the two cutters were racing back to England, two of the convict pirates, John Denner and Sam Thacker, had been found and arrested by Chinese officials. They had been living with fishermen in the Ryuku Islands when they had been discovered. Both men were escorted under armed guard to appear before the local magistrate. He received permission from the Governor of Fukien Provence to dispatch the two foreign prisoners to the Viceroy of Canton. The Viceroy of Canton made the decision based on the fact that the two prisoners were English to hold them under lock and key on the English ship *Samarang* for further questioning. The ship was not due to sail for some time; therefore, time was not of the essence.

Denner and Thacker gave false names as they explained they had been shipwrecked off Formosa in the brig *Edward*. The captain was suspicious of their story and he ordered the prisoners to be separated to await interrogation.

Coincidentally, a ship arrived in the harbour from Sydney, New South Wales, delivering among other things mail and newspapers including the *Sydney Gazette,* detailing the seizure by convict pirates of the *Cyprus* brig aka *Edward*.

Their cover was broken. Thacker maintained his original story but Denner made a full confession and turned informer. His statement was taken in detail he had ratted on all his fellow pirates hoping to save his own skin.

'I was not on deck when the mutiny occurred. I had gone below.'

'Who were the ringleaders of the mutiny?' asked the captain.

'Swallow was the main one and Jones and Templeman were by his side.'

'Was anybody killed during the mutiny?'

'Brown fell from the boom and drowned. Nobody else was seriously hurt.'

'You say there are four pirates on the *Charles Grant*. Where are the rest of them?'

'Seven decided not to go on and they were left on Niue Island in Tonga.'

'Is there anything else you wish to say in your defence?'

'Yes, sir. I was not a willing participant. I was coerced. I was ironed on board by the captain's orders.

'What was the captain's name?'

'Swallow, Captain William Swallow.'

'Why were you put in irons?'

'I tried to board an American whaler to get away.'

'You were obviously unsuccessful.'

'They pointed their muskets at me and ordered me back onboard.'

'How did you get to be living with the Chinese fishermen on Ryuku Island?'

'Thacker and I decided not to continue on in the brig. We both thought we had a better chance of survival with the fishermen.'

'Well, you were very much mistaken, weren't you? So your friend is called Thacker, is he?'

'Yes, sir, we both went under assumed names.'

'Right Denner, are you prepared to sign this statement?'

'I am, sir.'

The statement was signed on June 24 1830.

There were no ships sailing to either Sydney of London in the foreseeable future and as a consequence, the two pirates remained as prisoners on the *Samarang*.

Charles Grant
August 15 1830

William, as quartermaster, was at the wheel of the *Charles Grant*. From the first time he took control of the ship's wheel he admired everything about the magnificent clipper; its speed its manoeuvrability, the quality of the build— simply everything. He thought back to the *Cyprus* just before they scuttled her. The sails were ripped, the decks were filthy, there was a patch that was slowly leaking from the cannonball the Japanese fired yet he held fond memories of the brig. If it wasn't for her, he would labouring on Sarah Island under the strict rule of the British guards.

The trade winds were at strength, requiring Quartermaster Waldron to make frequent tacks and the ship responded beautifully.

William knew they were only three weeks away from berthing in London. He had no idea what or who awaited him on arrival but he hoped in wasn't the Thames Police.

He knew it wouldn't be Susan, his wife, and their two children as they had no idea he was returning home or the circumstances of his return. As far as Susan was concerned, her husband would be incarcerated in Australia for the remainder of his life, never to see his family again.

William Waldron aka Swallow was hopeful that Susan was still living in Whitechapel and he hoped the family could move away from London and possibly settle up north. This could only happen if he got away with his deception.

If he could take his family north to York, what would he do to earn a living?

William became quite morose; here he was at thirty-five; an escaped convict, mutineer and pirate. He should be a master of a ship such as the *Charles Grant* by now. He would have been as he was a skilled mariner however he stole some silver so that he could clothe and feed his family. His life and his ambitions changed forever on that day.

On the voyage home, the pirates sold various items, which had been pilfered from the *Cyprus,* to officers. Swallow sold his ornate writing desk.

All these items could link the pirates back to the seizure of the *Cyprus* but they didn't think it was a problem.

LONDON

CHAPTER 19

Captain Everest of the *Charles Grant* was happily sailing towards London, totally unaware the *Kellie Castle* had overtaken him and would arrive seven days ahead of the *Charles Grant* despite departing ten days later than his ship.

The *Kellie Castle* dropped anchor at Margate on August 30. All passengers were offloaded and taken to London by coach, thirty miles away. Also, mail and dispatches were taken to London.

Captain Finnegan sent a request for the Thames Police to send two officers to meet them at the East India dock to take custody of George Davis aka Huntley.

Two days of slow sailing saw the *Kellie Castle* berth at the East India dock. Waiting were members of the Thames Police, who took George into custody.

The police questioned George and although they had no physical evidence against him they did have a star witness; Billy Armstrong.

It was Billy's testimony that sealed George's fate.

September 7 1830

The *Charles Grant* arrived at Margate and anchored. Passengers were disembarked and dispatches and mail handed over to the correct authorities.

William Waldron approached his captain. 'Sir, may I request I leave the ship here?'

'For what reason, Waldron?'

'Sir, I am very keen to get to London as quickly as possible so that I can inform the owners of the fate of the *Edward*. They need to submit their insurance claim post haste.'

'Oh, I can understand that yes, by all means, leave now. Your pay and discharge papers will be at the East India office once we berth. Thank you for your service. You are an excellent quartermaster and I would be happy to write you a testimonial.'

'Thank you, sir, it's been a pleasure serving under you.'

Once ashore, Swallow kept low, not wanting to draw attention to himself. He used some of the money he had acquired selling the writing desk to travel to London. He waited for darkness before entering the Whitechapel precinct. He cautiously knocked on the front door of his wife's last known address, and a large burly fellow answered the door.

'Who are you and what do you want?'

'Forgive me for disturbing you, sir. I'm trying to find my wife, Susan Swallow.'

'She hasn't lived here for years.'

'Do you happen to know where she went?'

'No, I've got no idea.'

The fellow then closed the door in William's face.

How was he going to find his family?

At last the Charles Grant berthed at the East India Docks on September 9. Waiting were the Thames Police and all three convicts were arrested Watts, Beveridge and Stevenson.

In police custody the three gave their assumed names and maintained their story of being shipwrecked on the *Edward*. When asked what their captain's name was all three stated it was Waldron; not Swallow or Wilson.

The police decided to charge the three sailors with suspicion of felony, and they were remanded in custody awaiting further investigation.

At this early stage the police had no suspicion George Davis or the other three were connected with the seizure of the *Cyprus*. Their investigations related to the mystery of the *Edward* sinking. Billy's statement would change that.

Captain Waldron was being sought for questioning but could not be located; the police had hoped they would be able to grab him when he went to the East India offices to collect his pay, but he never picked it up. It seemed the elusive captain had vanished.

Without any concrete evidence to support the charge the police decided to free the four scoundrels.

Then, serendipity stepped in, and a witness came forward. His name was John Pobjoy. He knew the whole story and was more than willing to divulge it.

Great Britain was experiencing social change. The masses were being heard and in light of the French Revolution which only ended in 1799, the government of the day, the Tories led by the Duke of Wellington, decided they should act.

The penal code was reformed and over 200 minor offences were no longer punishable by death. Unfortunately for the escaped convicts, piracy wasn't one of them.

Other changes included allowing Catholics to vote and giving trade unions more freedom.

Also in 1830 King George IV died, succeeded by his brother King William IV. King William was a supporter of reform and his desire was to make England a more democratic nation.

Finally, general elections were held, with the Reform Party winning power.

So how did John Pobjoy end up in England? He worked his passage on a clipper. He arrived in July 1830, not long after the police arrested Davis, Watts and Stevenson.

Pobjoy had a few pounds to his name, but he had no permanent quarters and no longer knew anyone in London; he felt completely alone.

He knew that if he didn't find work there would be no alternative but to turn to his old trade, stealing.

It wasn't stealing that landed him in gaol, though; it was bashing a man that did not approve of Pobjoy's interest in his daughter.

Pobjoy was brought before the court and with the evidence against him the likely outcome would be gaol or even transportation back to New South Wales..

On the stand Pobjoy related to the magistrate how he saved the castaways at Recherche Bay.

'So you were being transported to Sarah Island, I take it?' said the magistrate.

'I was, Your Honour.'

'You took no part in the mutiny?'

'No, sir. I refused to join them.'

Pobjoy's story intrigued the magistrate and all the people in the court.

'I am impressed with the defendant's heroism and saving so many good people's lives. I don't condone his recent actions, but I am willing to discharge the charges on this instance. Mr Pobjoy; I don't want to see you before me again; if I do, I can assure you I won't be so lenient.'

'Yes, Your Honour. Thank you, Your Honour.

Pobjoy left the court. Skipping down the courthouse steps, he knew he had got away with one.

One of the policemen who arrested Pobjoy followed him out the court.

'Excuse me, Mr Pobjoy; may I have a word, please?'

'Oh dear, what are you going to nab me for now?'

'Nothing. I just want a word, that's all.'

'Right, about what?'

'We have four men in custody at the moment. I was wondering if you would be willing to look at them on the basis they may be pirates from the *Cyprus*.'

'Where are you holding them?'

'In the cells at Thames Police Station.'

'Right, I'll do it; if it is those bastards I'd gladly identify them. They gave me a lot of grief.

The policeman escorted Pobjoy to the police station and him down to the cells.

Pobjoy looked at the four men, all in one cell, and he immediately identified all four.

'Are you sure, Mr Pobjoy?'

'Bloody oath I'm sure. I spent enough time with them.'

'Would you be willing to swear in a court of law?'

'I will. No problem there.'

'Can I ask you to come back tomorrow and meet my supervisor and relate to him what you've told me?'

'Certainly. What time would you like to see me?'

'Let's say 10 am.'

'I'll be here.'

John Pobjoy was good for his word. He arrived at the Thames Police Station at 10 am on the dot.

He was greeted by the policeman who spoke to him the day before. His name was Ferguson, which John though ironic. He was invited into the supervisor's office.

'Well. Mr Pobjoy, I believe you have identified the four prisoners we are holding on suspicion?'

'Yes, sir, that's correct.'

'The problem I have with your testimony is that you are an ex-convict who was transported to the colonies for fourteen years.'

'That's right, but I did receive a full pardon for saving the castaways' lives.'

'Yes, I'm aware of that; very commendable I must say.'

'Sir, I know what you're saying. My background might be used against me. I can suggest a way of proving the truth of it.'

'How so?'

'On the ship that brought me back to England was Mr Thomas Capon. He was Head Gaoler of Hobart Town. He would be able to identify the culprits.'

The police were able to locate Mr Capon in London. He was shown the four convicts and was able to identify all four as convicts that were on board the *Cyprus* when it sailed for Sarah Island

Both witnesses gave their statements to the police magistrate. The pirates were in deep trouble.

Do You Take This Woman?

Chapter 20

The only pirate on the loose was Captain Waldron aka Swallow. No matter how hard they looked or what tactics they employed he evaded the law. They even posted a wanted notice in the *Hue and Cry*, a paper preferred by criminals.

Swallow had taken yet another pseudonym and he was now William Todd.

Swallow had dreamed of seeing his wife and children again. It was what kept him going while captain of the brig sailing halfway around the world.

He had a difficult task ahead; he needed to avoid the police but at the same time, he needed to see his family again. He couldn't use his old criminal network, as they would surely snitch on him for the reward.

William's money was fast running out. He knew he must raise more money to exist and hide from the law. He decided to sell some of the items he brought ashore when he arrived back. The accepted method was going to a pawnbroker. He was able to raise a few pounds from the pledge. He decided he needed to take up his speciality of tier ranging again if he was to survive.

Tier ranging encompassed pilfering cargo from ships moored in the Thames. This activity would be conducted after dark. The next step would be selling the goods to pawnbrokers.

The pawnbrokers knew every criminal in London and had a better information network than the police. It was with this in mind that William began asking about the whereabouts of his wife.

A few weeks later he discovered his wife Susan was now living in a slum in Lambeth in South London. He was excited at the prospect of seeing his beloved family again; something he thought would never happen.

He found the dilapidated house and waited until nightfall. He was extremely nervous when he knocked on the front door.

'Hello, Susan, my love, I bet you thought you would never see me again.'

'My God, William; is it really you?'

'It is, my darling. I'm back; I missed you, love, I won't leave you again, I promise. How are the children?'

'They're well; they're living with my parents. I thought you were dead. I was told they hanged you. William, I've married again. My husband is inside.'

'I don't believe it. How could you go and do that?'

'I'm sorry. I thought you were dead.'

'Where's your so-called husband now?'

'He's inside. Don't hurt him, William, he's a good man.'

'Good or bad, I want to speak to him. What's his name?'

'Tom Fluke.'

'What's he do for a living to keep you in this luxury?'

'He's a grocer's assistant.'

'What, he sells vegetables?'

'William, he's been very good to me.'

'All right, well let's meet him then.'

Susan allowed Swallow into her slum-like residence and led him through to the kitchen to where Tom was making a cup of tea.

'So who was at the front door, darling?'

'It was me.'

Tom quickly turned around only to see William Swallow…not that he knew who this fellow was.

'And who are you, pray tell?'

'I'm William Swallow. Susan's legal husband.'

'Oh, my God! We thought you were dead.'

'So I gather.'

'How did you get back to England?'

'Never mind how I got here. The point is, I'm still married to Susan and you're not. Not legally anyway. You two could be up on bigamy charges.'

'So what do you want me to do?'

'I don't really care. I know what I'm going to do, I'm taking Susan with me and we'll live together as man and wife once more.'

'You can't do that.'

'Really? Just watch me. Susan, grab your things. We're going back to my place.'

'Are you sure we should be doing this?'

'Of course I am. You're my wife, for God's sake.'

I don't have much to bring.'

'Don't you worry, darling, that'll soon change.'

The pair disappeared into the night, leaving a bewildered Tom Fluke to ponder his future without Susan, the woman he loved.

William's address was 31 Isabella Street in Southwark. It was a district the police avoided if they could.

Isabella Street

This was where William and Susan reacquainted themselves in every sense of the word.

When William decided to take a stroll, he passed the local shop and decided to buy a copy of *Hue and Cry*. He read it as he walked along and suddenly an article leaped out, grabbing his attention.

Cyprus Pirates Arrested

He read that Davis, Watts, Stevenson and Beveridge had been arrested and were awaiting trial. He knew it would only be a matter of time before the bobbies found him.

He returned home, only to find Tom Fluke.

'What are you doing here, Fluke?'

'I came to tell you the police are sniffing around the neighbourhood.'

'And what are they sniffing?'

'I've been informed that a few people have told them that Susan is living with another man. I don't think they will take long to figure you're the other man.'

'Well, they haven't found me yet, and with God's blessing they won't.'

'It's not you they're looking for, Swallow. They know you are too slippery. It's Susan they want.'

'Why her?'

'Because they know if they find her, they'll find you.'

'Fuck it! I suppose I should let her go home with you out of harm's way. The last thing I want for her is to be put in gaol or transported for bigamy.'

With great sadness, he said goodbye to his beloved wife Susan. He was now on his own again, saddened by his loss but determined not to be caught by the constabulary.

Have Your Day in Court

Chapter 21

After their arrest, the suspected pirates were kept in custody for over a month. The authorities hoped they would capture William Swallow, the captain of the *Cyprus,* enabling all five to be tried together. The police had not been successful in apprehending the scoundrel; therefore, it was decided to go ahead and try the four.

October 13 1830
Thames Police Court

Two policemen escorted the four men into the dock. The magistrate hearing the case was Mr Ballantine, known to be a liberal law reformer. He was opposed to thousands of the poor being tried for minor crimes and being gaoled or transported. Some were even sentenced to death.

The charge laid against the four men was:

'Being concerned in the seizure of the colonial brig *Cyprus*, between Hobart Town and Macquarie Harbour, in the month of August 1829 after overpowering and wounding the military guard.'

None of the men had legal representation except Davis, who was being supported by his family.

One of the reforms Mr Ballantine supported was ensuring that all citizens had legal counsel.

Clandestinely, the magistrate paid for the other three to be represented by a barrister.

The public gallery was completely full. There were even interested spectators in the street outside the courthouse. The story of transported convicts escaping by seizing one of His Majesty's brigs fuelled the imagination of the public.

John Pobjoy was feeling very nervous. The only times he'd been in court were when he had been charged with various offences.

The police were very protective of their star witness. They had accommodated him in a safe house for the past month. He received a small allowance to purchase food and other essentials, and he hoped he would receive a sizeable reward once the pirates were convicted.

Once the hearing got underway, the prisoner's counsel advised the court that they did not intend to cross-examine the prosecution's witnesses. However, they would reserve their defence.

The first witness was Thomas Capon, former Head Gaoler of Hobart Town.

'Mr Capon, I believe you knew the four accused when in Hobart Town,' said the prosecution barrister.

'Yes, sir. I did.'

'May I ask how you knew four convicts who were not residing in Hobart Town?'

'I recognised them from when they were brought to Hobart Town en route to Sarah Island.'

'There must have been hundreds if not thousands of convicts who pass through Hobart Town.'

'Yes, there were, sir, but I never forget a face and all four prisoners embarked on the *Cyprus* bound for Sarah Island. Of that I'm sure.'

'Thank you, Mr Capon. You may step down.'

The next witness was John Pobjoy and as he entered the witness stand the four accused glared at the weasel of a man.

'Mr Pobjoy, do you know the accused?' asked the prosecution counsel.

'Yes, I do.'

'Could you tell the court how you became acquainted with the four men standing in the dock'?

'I was on the *Cyprus* with them we were all being transported to Sarah Island.'

'Are you aware if the four accused took part in the seizure of the *Cyprus*?'

'Sir, all four were active and enthusiastic participants.'

'Did you see if they were armed?'

'Yes, each man was carrying a musket stolen from the guards.'

'What's your recollection of that day?'

Pobjoy described how the convicts took over the ship and fourteen of them along with the accused sailed off. The passengers and guards plus the brig's crew were abandoned on a desolate beach at Recherche Bay.

There were several convicts, including Pobjoy, who refused to go with the mutineers they too were dumped on the beach.

Pobjoy was enjoying the limelight. He knew most of the newspapers were in the public gallery.

He went on to describe his heroic actions to save the castaways; no mention of Morgan was made.

'Thank you, Mr Pobjoy. You may stand down.'

' Your Honour, I would like to call the next witness, Captain Everest, Master of the *Charles Grant*.

'Captain Everest, can you identify the four men standing in the dock?'

'Yes, I can; my ship took three of them on as they intimated they had been shipwrecked while sailing on the brig *Edward*. All three worked as crew during the journey from Canton, China, to England. An additional man who was the captain of the *Edward* was appointed as quartermaster. He was an excellent mariner whose name was Waldron.'

'It is my understanding that some of your officers in good faith purchased various items from the shipwrecked sailors. I would like to present these items as exhibits and ask Mr Pobjoy to identify them as belonging to the *Cyprus*,' said the prosecutor.

'Mr Pobjoy, do you recognise any of these articles as belonging to the *Cyprus*?'

'Yes, sir, I can. I believe they all belonged to the *Cyprus*.'

'It is my understanding you were taken to where the longboat used by the accused is currently housed and identified her as being the boat belonging to the *Cyprus*?'

'That is correct, sir.'

'Thank you, Mr Pobjoy. You can stand down.'

As Pobjoy walked past the prisoners they all glared at him. If they hadn't been restrained, they would have killed him.

'Your Honour, I call Billy Armstrong to the stand.'

A very nervous Billy took the stand.

'I understand you sailed on the *Kellie Castle* from Canton to England?'

'Yes, sir. I did.'

'I also believe you befriended George Davis who was also sailing on the *Kellie Castle*.'

'Yes, sir.'

'Did George Davis confess to you his role in the seizure of the brig

Cyprus?'

'Yes, he did a full confession.'

'What did he say to you?'

'He told me he helped overcome the guards and stole their muskets and how exciting it all was.'

'Thank you, Billy; you may step down.'

The young seaman walked sheepishly past the dock, trying to avoid eye contact with George.

The magistrate, having considered the evidence, committed the four accused to stand trial at the Admiralty Court.

THE ADMIRALTY
WHITEHALL

The magistrate also ruled the four prisoners should receive their wages from the East India company for the passage from China to England. He was concerned they would not be able to pay for a defence counsel if they were not remunerated.

The prisoners did not have to wait long for they were back in court the following day.

Once again the trial attracted a large crowd, news of the pirates' amazing exploits having been reported in several newspapers, including *The Times*.

Tom Fluke considered turning Swallow in to the police, but he decided not to. The pirate could have reported him and Susan to the authorities anonymously, and they would have been arrested for bigamy; a very serious charge indeed.

Fluke knew Susan still visited her husband in Isabella Street on a regular basis, but he also knew he just had to accept it as after all, they were still man and wife.

It didn't stop him moaning about it he opened up to a close friend in the local pub one night. The friend's name was Harry Taylor.

Harry saw an opportunity. As a street barrow man, he didn't earn much money and the reward would come in handy. He made a visit to the local police station where the bobbies were very keen to know Sparrow's whereabouts. They were not, however, keen enough to go into Isabella Street at night.

The police arranged for Taylor to park his barrow outside the house next morning.

October 15 1830

It was a Friday morning. William was sitting at his kitchen table drinking a cup of tea, and waiting for Susan to arrive back from the store. He heard a crashing noise.

Constables Goding and Drew had broken down the front door and before he knew it he was in manacles again and led away.

SWALLOW IN A BIRDCAGE

CHAPTER 21

Swallow wasn't in the holding cell for long. At 9 pm on Friday, he appeared in the Thames Police Court before Captain Ritchbell, the sitting magistrate.

No. 1010. Thames Police Court, Arbour Square, Stepney.

He was charged with being involved in the mutiny and seizure of the colonial brig *Cyprus*.

He had no legal representation and the other four prisoners were unaware of his capture.

The reason for the late sitting was to identify Swallow and remand him to the following day.

When the magistrate asked him if he was guilty or not guilty and Swallow responded in a clear and loud voice: 'Not Guilty.'

A policeman involved in Swallow's capture was asked to give evidence of Swallow's arrest.

Swallow's previous criminal record was also given to the court. All the details were recorded by the Clerk of the Court, thus becoming a public document, which was available to the newspapers to report.

The usual protocol was that the previous criminal record is only available once the jury has brought down their verdict. Having this information could influence their decision.

The reason the court accepted Swallow's previous record was the need to prove that the man standing in the dock had been transported to Van Diemen's Land as a convict. The fact that William had no legal representation meant there was no objection to citing his record.

The police made it known that Swallow was a desperate criminal who had been in trouble with the law since a young age.

The final bit of evidence was that he had been convicted in 1828 of a capital offence and sentenced to hang. His sentence was commuted to transportation for life.

Mention was also made of Tom Fluke and Susan Swallow's illegal marriage, but no charges were intended.

The information divulged to the court was more than was needed to identify Swallow. It was meant to paint a picture of a hardened criminal that deserved no mercy. Despite some of the information being false the newspapers would report it verbatim.

Despite the lateness of the hour, Swallow announced to the court he wishes to make a full confession of the role he played in the seizure of the *Cyprus*.

'Do you realise, Mr Swallow, you are under no obligation to confess and in fact, I advise you strongly against it?' suggested the magistrate.

'I understand, Your Honour, however, I insist I am given the opportunity to confess.'

'Very well if you insist, although once again I advise you are entering dangerous territory.'

Swallow began his extensive precise and logical defence, which the Clerk of the Court recorded meticulously. When the magistrate started to nod off, he adjourned the sitting until the following morning. The clock in the courtroom showed it was past midnight.

Swallow knew that every word of his confession would be reported in all the London newspapers. His cunning would elicit public sympathy for the pirate king.

Swallow discarded his normal rights, including avoiding answers which might incriminate him. Usually, the accused said nothing except *guilty* or *not guilty*. It was the lawyers who did all the talking. After all, that was what they

109

were paid for.

On Saturday morning, the court reconvened under a different magistrate; Mr Broderip. Captain Ritchbell was also present. Before Swallow could continue, Mr Broderip warned him against doing so. 'It is fraught with danger,' he advised.

'Your Honour, I would like to continue.'

'Very well.'

There wasn't a spare seat in the court and as before a large crowd had assembled outside.

Swallow revelled in the attention. He knew it would help his case.

For the next three hours, Swallow dictated his statement to the clerk. He was concise and used his words wisely.

It was obvious that the public gallery were intrigued in William's story. Some were living their life through Swallow; the life they would never experience.

Swallow was brilliant. He told his story without repeating a word or fumbling over facts. Surely it was the most lucid defence ever by a prisoner.

Swallow's story revolved around the fact he was forced to join the mutineers, as he was the only one who knew how to sail and navigate such a ship. He was threatened with death if he did not agree.

Normally, such a proposition would have been thrown out of court, however Swallow's eloquence and convincing narrative made the story almost believable.

Swallow continued with his statement.

'The reason the men seized the *Cyprus* and sailed away was to avoid becoming a slave on Sarah Island. The treatment we all received in New South Wales was appalling. We all received the cat several times a year, hence our backs lay testimony to the cruelty of such a punishment.

'The authorities told us that Sarah Island would be twice as hard.'

Convicts at Sarah Island

Great Britain had entered an age of liberalism. For example, the number of capital crimes had been reduced dramatically.

Swallow's statement about the harsh punishment inflicted on convicts was designed to influence the jury and the public in favour of the five men on trial, including himself.

'Although the charges do not mention piracy, there is no doubt it will be alleged. I would like to point out that the *Cyprus* was seized without loss of life. The men on the *Cyprus* did not undertake any predatory actions against any other vessels despite numerous opportunities to do so. There were no new crimes committed by the convicts during the entire voyage.'

Wednesday 20 October

For the first time since returning to England, all five convicts were assembled in the dock. The primary purpose was to take evidence against William Swallow. All five nodded to each other, silently acknowledging their predicament.

The sitting magistrate was Mr Ballantine and the only defence counsel present was Mr Wooler, representing George Davis.

John Pobjoy entered the witness box. The prosecutor began directing questions to the star witness.

'Mr Pobjoy, how would you describe Mr Swallow's actions on the day of the seizure of the *Cyprus*?'

'He was very much involved, sir. He was directing the other convicts what to do. I would suggest he was the main ringleader.'

'Mr Swallow, as you are representing yourself you are permitted to cross-examine the witness.'

'Thank you, Your Honour. Your Honour, Pobjoy is a lying scoundrel. I believe he has committed perjury and should be punished for it. Far from directing the seizure as Pobjoy alludes to it, I was in fact below decks as I was very ill when the brig was seized.

'I was dragged up to take control of the ship as I was the only mariner aboard.'

The prosecutor asked Pobjoy a question.

'Was Swallow indeed below decks and under the care of the ship's doctor when the *Cyprus* was seized?'

'He had certainly been in the doctor's hands on the day before the mutiny. However, he was very active and quite well when the brig was seized. As I stated before, I believe he was the principal ringleader.'

'Liar,' shouted Swallow.

'Order,' said the magistrate.

After Swallow's outburst, several crew and officers of the *Charles Grant* gave evidence identifying Swallow as having worked his passage home using the name Captain Waldron. They also testified Captain Waldron had sold various items while on board.

Several items were tendered by the police as having been stolen from ships moored in the Thames, proving Swallow was a thief.

The magistrate announced that he would be approaching the East India Company for Swallow's wages while working on the Charles Grant, so that Swallow could employ counsel.

He then declared, 'The charge of mutiny and piracy, in running away with the brig and cargo, has been made out against the five prisoners. I commit them for trial at the Admiralty Sessions, at the Old Bailey, which will commence on Monday next.'

Swallow was correct. The term *piracy* was now mentioned in the charge.

THE OLD BAILEY

TRIALS & TRIBULATIONS

CHAPTER 22

The Old Bailey 1830

November 4 1830

The five accused were standing in the dock as the indictment against them was read to the court.

The accused piratically and feloniously setting upon breaking and entering a certain brig called the CYPRUS, the property of our late Lord the King upon the high sea(sic) within the jurisdiction of the Admiralty of England and piratically beating and wounding John Pobjoy and other mariners lawfully on board the said ship and piratically and feloniously stealing and running away with the said ship and the boat's apparel, tackle and furniture thereof value £2000 the property of our Lord the late King.

113

The presiding judge was Lord Justice Bolland. To assist him was a nautical law specialist and a Senior Judge at Admiralty Sessions, Justice Sir Charles Robinson.

A jury of twelve citizens, all men, were sworn in.

There were three counsels for the prosecution: Mr Wightman, Dr Jenner and Mr Adolphus.

The defence comprised three counsels also.

John Pobjoy was called to the witness stand to be examined by Mr Adolphus.

Pobjoy recounted the events at Recherche Bay.

'Mr Pobjoy, can you describe what part the five accused played in the seizure of the brig?'

'My recollection is Swallow complained to me that he had been forced to take part in the mutiny by the convicts. His conduct was by no means as bad as the others.'

'Was Swallow armed during the mutiny?'

'No sir, neither he nor Stevenson was armed.'

'So who were armed?'

'All the other mutineers to a man, sir.'

114

'What weapons did they carry?'

'Muskets, pistols even bayonets.'

'What involvement did Swallow have in the seizure?'

'I saw him slackening the anchor chain and breaking the locks on the hatches with an axe.'

'Thank you, Mr Pobjoy, you may step down.'

The court calls George Davis to the stand.

'You have heard Mr Pobjoy's testimony. What is your recollection of the event?'

'Pobjoy is a liar. He was armed with a musket throughout the seizure and he acted as a sentry on the deck of the *Cyprus* after the mutiny. The little weasel got cold feet and swam ashore to join the passengers on the beach.'

'What role did Watts play?'

'He took the passengers ashore in the longboat. He made several trips and he then returned to the brig.'

Pobjoy was brought back to the stand to clarify a few details of his testimony.

It would seem Pobjoy had deliberately tried to incriminate Davis and Watts and to exculpate Swallow, Stevenson and Beveridge.

Davis's counsel then cross-examined Pobjoy.

'Mr Pobjoy, would you describe yourself as a law abiding citizen?' asked Mr Phillips, representing Davis.

'I am now.'

'What about before now?'

'Well, it's on the public record that I was transported to the colonies for fourteen years but I received a full pardon for my efforts in saving the castaways at Recherche Bay.'

'Yes, I understand you had already served thirteen years when you received your pardon.'

'That's right.'

'Would you regard yourself of being a model prisoner?'

'Maybe not a model prisoner, but better than most.'

'I believe you committed a number of offences while you were incarcerated. Were you ever flogged?'

'Yes, I received a few lashes. Everybody did.'

'How many lashes exactly, Mr Pobjoy?'

'I don't remember.'

'Let me refresh your memory. You received 200 lashes with the cat o' nine tails. That's more than just a few.'

'As I said, everybody received a visit by the cat.'

'Why were you sent to Macquarie Harbour?'

'I went as a volunteer.'

' I can't imagine anybody volunteering to go to that hellhole. You went there as a spy, didn't you?'

'Yes.'

'Who were you going to spy on; your fellow convicts?'

'That's right.'

'Thank you, Your Honour, I have no further questions.'

Swallow's counsel, Mr Bodkin, asked more questions of Mr Pobjoy.

'Did you hear Swallow say that he was forced by the mutineers to navigate the vessel?'

'Yes.'

Was Swallow ill at the time of the mutiny?'

'Yes, he was very ill.'

'Thank you, Your Honour, no further questions.'

The Crown made the decision not to call Pobjoy to the stand again as he had proved to be an unreliable witness, contradicting the evidence he gave in the police court.

Pobjoy was relieved that he was no longer required.

The reason for his change in testimony is not really known, but the speculation was that he realised the gravity of the situation. He would have been instrumental in sending men to the gallows.

He was also fearful that the citizens of London would accurse him forever.

Davis and Watts were in real jeopardy of climbing the thirteen steps to be met by their executioner.

Swallow's situation looked much brighter.

The prosecution called their next witness, Doctor Walter Williams, the ship's doctor on the *Cyprus*. He had been away from London while the committal hearing had taken place and had only arrived back recently.

The magistrates had not examined him.

'Dr Williams, can you identify the men standing in the dock?'

'No, not all of them. I can identify Swallow and Watts.'

'Are you aware of what roles these two men played in the seizure of the brig?'

'I know Watts was on deck. He was armed and took an active role in the mutiny.'

'What about Swallow?'

'I overheard him say to some officers being loaded into the longboat, 'you see gentlemen I am a pressed man. I am unarmed, surrounded by armed men. I also saw Swallow retrieve some blankets for Mrs Carew but Watts forbade it.'

' Did you treat Swallow for any illness around the time of the mutiny?'

'Yes, he had been affected by a dangerous complaint although he was recovering at the time of the mutiny.'

Swallow must have been elated that his fake illness had fooled the good doctor.

Mr Phillips cross-examined the witness hoping he could extract something from the doctor, but his answers were vague and unhelpful.

The next defence counsel to cross-examine Dr Williams was Mr Clarkson.

'Doctor, did you notice a man called Ferguson on the deck at the time of the mutiny?'

'Yes, I did. He seemed to be the ringleader.'

'Were the others acting under his control?'

'They may have been under his control. I'm not really sure.'

'Thank you, Doctor Williams, you may step down.'

The next witness called was Mr Thomas Capon, Head Gaoler of Hobart Town.

'Mr Capon, can you identify the five prisoners in the dock?'

'No, I cannot say whether they were convicts.'

' Are you positive?'

'No, but I cannot say I recognise them.'

Capon's evidence was contrary to the evidence he gave in the police court.

The defence decided not to cross-examine.

'Thank you, Mr Capon. You may step down.'

The case for the Crown concluded with evidence from officers of the *Charles Grant* and *Kellie Castle* on the manner in which the five accused had returned to England.

'The accused are permitted to make unsworn statements in their defence if they so wish to.'

Only Swallow spoke.

'Gentlemen I was forced to remain on board the brig.'

Lord Justice Bolland summed up the evidence and he warned the jury to disregard all evidence except that which they heard in the court.

He also instructed that if they had any doubts of the guilt of any prisoners, they should find a verdict of not guilty. He stressed that it was irrelevant whether the prisoners had been convicts at the time of the alleged offence.

'Gentlemen of the jury, consider your verdict.'

The twelve men of the jury filed out to consider their verdict. Two and a half hours later, they returned.

The five accused all looked nervous; some more than others. Swallow seemed the calmest of them all.

The foreman of the jury stood and announced the verdicts:

George Davis	Guilty
William Watts	Guilty
Alexander Stevenson	Guilty, but recommended to the merciful consideration of the court, on the grounds that he was not as active as others in the mutiny.
John Beveridge	Guilty, but recommended to the merciful consideration of the court, on the grounds that he was not as active as others in the mutiny.
William Swallow	Not Guilty

William was ecstatic; he had fooled the court with his statement of innocence. He could no longer be tried for piracy despite what new evidence may emerge.

There was, however, the charge of, "illegally returning from transportation" to face. This was also a capital offence so he may yet face the hangman.

He wished he had surrendered to the authorities in China. If he had, he wouldn't be facing this serious charge.

Still, he was in a much better situation than his four comrades.

Stevenson and Beveridge would be sentenced to hang, but it was highly likely the Executive Council would commute the sentence to a long prison sentence.

The judge asked the customary question:

Have you anything to say…?

They were all silent.

Sir Charles Robinson had the solemn duty of sentencing the four to death.

He put the black cloth over his wig and pronounced the words every prisoner dreads.

George James Davis alias, Huntley; William Watts alias, Charles Williams; Alexander Stevenson alias, Tetford and John Beveridge, alias Anderson; the sentence of the Court is that you be taken from hence from the place you whence you came, and from thence, on a day to be appointed by the Executive Council of His Majesty's Government, to a place of execution, and there you shall, each and every one of you, be hanged by the neck until you are dead: and may God have mercy on your souls.

The prisoners were taken down to the cells to await their transfer to Newgate Prison.

'This is all your fucking fault, Davis. If you hadn't let the cat out of the bag we would all still be free,' said Watts.

'I know. I'm sorry, mates.'

'We're not your fucking mates.'

'Oh well, I suppose it was always going to end like this.'

'Didn't have to.'

The sound of the police arriving to take them the short distance to Newgate Prison ended the conversation.

One Down One to Go

Chapter 23

William Swallow was not a free man; he was sitting in his damp cell at Newgate prison awaiting his next trial. If convicted he could either be hanged or more likely transported back to Van Diemen's Land. He was not sure which would be preferable—being executed or living a life of floggings and hard labour for the remainder of his life.

He had survived all his life thus far on his cunning, courage and determination. He had always had the gift of the gab, talking his way out of many difficult situations.

He decided to write a comprehensive confession based on his success with the first one at his trial in the Police Court.

This confession ignored the welfare of his comrades sentenced to hang.

The confession was in the form of a letter to the Home Secretary, detailing every detail of the seizure of the *Cyprus*. It was the Home Secretary who would be considering his companions' appeals and Swallow's letter would not help their case at all. Swallow could not care less. He was only interested in his own welfare.

The eight-page letter was half fact and half fiction, detailing his early life through to his current age of thirty-eight. Naturally, the seizure and subsequent voyage were detailed in detail. In his first confession, he testified a Japanese cannonball had sunk the brig. In his subsequent confession he described how Davis and Jones and another he could not recall went down into the ship's hold, cut away her sealing and two of her timber boards.

'They then returned to the deck, and told me what they had done.'

Swallow's most damning and treasonous act was to confess it was the Niue Islands and not Hawaii as previously stated where the seven convicts were living. He even suggested a ship from Sydney could sail to Niue and pick up Ferguson and the other mutineers.

Finally, he ended his narrative:

'I am now, Honourable Sir, detained in Newgate for the purpose of taking my trial for returning from transportation before my time was complete. I do hope that when you consider that I was not brought here by any premeditated act of my own, and consider also the privations I have already suffered and taking all other circumstances; my age being now 45 (actually 38) and my wife and daughter; into your humane consideration, you will allow me, if not my enlargement, as moderate fine as the case may deserve.

I am Sir,

Your very obedient humble servant

and unfortunate prisoner

William Swallow

alias William Waldron

John Pobjoy also felt he had been badly done by. His three shillings' sustenance allowance ceased once the trial had been completed. He had been hoping for a sizeable reward but no mention of it was made.

He petitioned the then Prime Minister, Sir Robert Peel, reiterating the role he played in saving forty women children and men from certain starvation.

He received no reply.

He was elated when he received a letter from the Chief of Police informing him that expenses due to him for his duties as a witness were now to be paid.

John Pobjoy arrived at Police Headquarters ever hopeful he would be informed of the amount of his reward.

He waited in the anteroom of the Police Chief for fifteen minutes he was then shown into the grand office by a constable.

'Good afternoon, Mr Pobjoy.'

'Good afternoon, sir.'

'Well, down to business. I have the amount of £5 to give you for your expenses. I need you to sign a receipt if you could.'

'Yes, certainly.'

Pobjoy dutifully signed the receipt with an X.

'Sir, may inquire when I will receive my reward and the amount of said reward?'

'I'm sorry, Mr Pobjoy, but there will be no further payment to you other than the £5 received.'

'If it wasn't for me, you would never have got a conviction.'

'I agree and we appreciate your efforts. Now if you'll excuse me.'

'I'm going to take this to a higher authority.'

'Do as you will, Mr Pobjoy but you have signed the receipt which precludes you from receiving any more compensation. The constable will show you out.'

Pobjoy left the Police Chief's office a dejected man.

He petitioned the Duke of Wellington but to no avail.

The petition was forwarded to the Home Department for Lord Melbourne's consideration.

Pobjoy tried to elevate the urgency of his plea by writing to Lord Melbourne personally.

He received no reply.

December 8 1830

The Executive Council met to consider the case of the four pirates condemned to death.

It had been four weeks since the court had sentenced them to hang.

After due consideration and discussion, it was decided that Davis and Watts should hang. The date of execution was fixed at 16 December.

Stevenson and Beveridge had their initial sentence commuted to Transportation for Life.

Swallow was to stand trial on the charge of having *illegally returned from transportation*. He pleaded guilty to the charge, relying on his petition to the Home Secretary to receive a reprieve.

If only they had all stayed in Tonga and enjoyed the good life instead of putting everything on the line, including their lives, to return to Mother England!

Swallow was also sentenced to hang, but the Home Secretary reprieved him and he was sentenced to transportation for life.

The petition he so meticulously wrote was filed away in the Home Office archives. It had a notation attached.

Character very bad. Was concerned in seizing the Cyprus on her passage from Van Diemen's Land to a penal settlement.

Of the five pirates who returned to the bosom of their motherland, two would be hanged and three would be transported back to the hell they had come from.

The reigning monarch of the day was King William IV, also known affectionately by his subjects as King Billy. He married Princess Adelaide of Saxe-Meiningen of Germany.

They had no children and therefore the heir to the throne was Princess Victoria, then only eleven years of age

King William was regarded as a Constitutional Monarch and would only act on the advice of his ministers. It was with this in mind that John Pobjoy wrote a letter of appeal to Queen Adelaide. Pobjoy was full of remorse for damning his fellow prisoners to hang.

The last paragraph of his letter stated:

Majesty to beg, earnestly beg, our beloved King, George Davis and William Watts, which must still further raise Your Majesty in the estimation of your affectionate people, as well as confer a deep and lasting obligation on their prosecutor and Your Majesty's
Devoted
Humble
Subject and
Servant John Pobjoy late of His Majesty's Brig Cyprus

Pobjoy signed with an X, he was illiterate and used the services of a scrivener for all his correspondence.

Pobjoy ignored the normal protocols and hand-delivered the letter to St James's Palace where the queen was in residence at the time.

The queen did not respond to Pobjoy's plea and his letters were forwarded to the Home Office along with all the other documents pertaining to the seizure of the *Cyprus*.

Pobjoy continued his mission to save Davis and Watts from the hangman's noose.

He approached the Lord Mayor of London, Alderman J Key, a magistrate by profession.

Friends had advised him that the Lord Mayor had considerable influence in government circles.

Pobjoy admitted that his evidence had not been truthful. Swallow had been the ringleader and Watts and Davis had no more involvement in the mutiny than Stevenson and Beveridge.

The Lord Mayor agreed to take Pobjoy's depositions and forward them to the appropriate authorities.

He forwarded them to the Home Secretary, Lord Melbourne. He then, in turn, passed them on to the Sheriff of London who was the officer responsible for the executions. The Sheriff showed the affidavit to the foreman of the jury at the trial, Mr James Nott. He then spoke to other members of the jury three of which signed a Petition of Royal Mercy.

The petition remained unanswered. Whether the king read the affidavit is unclear. The Sheriff was obliged to do his duty and arrange the execution of the two condemned pirates.

EXECUTION DOCK

LAST PORT OF CALL

CHAPTER 24

Execution Dock on the banks of the Thames was the traditional place where pirates and other seafarers were hanged. It had been the site of executions for over four hundred years.

One of the most infamous was Captain Kidd who was "hanged in chains" another term for this gruesome practice gibbeting.

He remained on the banks of the Thames for three years for all to see.

December 16 1830

It was a cold dreary day in London when Davis and Watts were loaded onto a cart at Newgate Prison to undergo the short trip to Execution Dock. The Sheriff of London and an entourage of officials accompanied them in a procession of black carriages.

The fact that Christmas was only a week away was not lost on the two condemned men.

When they reached the execution site both climbed the steps of the gallows to meet their executioner.

Both were asked if they had anything to say and both men declared it was Swallow and Ferguson who initiated the mutiny.

'If anyone is not guilty it is Beveridge and Stevenson; they were pressed into the act against their will.'

Both Davis and Watts said their prayers then they dropped into eternity.

They were the last pirates hanged.

Four years later Execution Dock was closed.

Beveridge and Stevenson tried their hardest to get a reprieve. They hired a scrivener as both were illiterate. They modelled their petition on Pobjoy's and Swallow's statement hoping King William IV would read it and offer a Royal Pardon.

They received no such pardon, not even an acknowledgment that the king had received it, let alone read it.

December 31 1831

Swallow, Beveridge and Stevenson were put on board the *Argyle* bound for Van Diemen's Land.

All three convicts knew what to expect as they had all experienced the hardships of transportation before.

"The Three Pirates of the *Cyprus*" was how the other prisoners referred to the three. They were regarded as role models. There wasn't a prisoner on their deck who didn't want to hear about their adventures, particularly in Tonga.

128

Five pirates were accounted for but what happened to the rest?

Ferguson, Lynch, Templeton, Briant and Towers all escaped from Niue before a British warship, the *Zebra,* could pick them up. It was thought they got to America.

Herring, Jones and Pennell last heard of leaving Canton on the Danish brig *Pulen,* bound for New Orleans.

Thacker escaped from custody en route to Sydney and was never heard of again.

These men escaped the tyranny of being a convict, slaving away in the world's toughest prisons.

Not all the pirates were that fortunate.

Brown died while passing through the South and North Islands of New Zealand. He fell from the mast and drowned at sea.

Davis and Watts had been hanged in chains at Execution Dock.

Camm was recaptured, tried, and hanged in Hobart.

McGuire received a life sentence on Norfolk Island, a hellhole worse than Sarah Island.

Beveridge, Denner and Stevenson became prisoners on Sarah Island.

Swallow, who planned the mutiny but was found innocent, was also sent to Sarah Island.

Swallow and his crew were an inspiration to others who had aspirations of escape by sea.

BOOK TWO

THE TRUE ADVENTURES OF CAPTAIN JAMES PORTER

CHAPTER 1

Swallow's task each day was logging timber, including Huon pine, for shipbuilding. It was backbreaking work. Governor Arthur instructed the administration on Sarah Island that the prisoners who seized the *Cyprus* would be classified as hard labour convicts.

One convict who befriended Swallow was James Porter. He too was a seafarer. The only time convicts could talk was after dark when they were locked in their austere, cold quarters. James would ask William about crossing the Pacific in a relatively small ship.

James Porter was ten years younger than William Swallow, but they had similar backgrounds. Swallow was raised in the slums of Whitechapel whereas Porter was born and raised in Bermondsey, also a slum in South-East London.

Bermondsey

London was not a nice place to grow up if you were poor; the stench of open sewers permeated the air. The sewers were also used for drinking water; hence cholera was prolific. Crime was rampant many of the convicts who were transported came from the Bermondsey area.

When Porter was ten years old, John Bellingham who had grievances with the government, assassinated Prime Minister Spencer Perceval. He was tried and convicted and sentenced to hang. Thousands of London citizens attended the execution to show their support for the condemned man. Such was the mood in England at the time that many sought a revolution similar to the French Revolution. The new monarch, the king's son, had taken the title George IV when his father George III was deemed incapable to rule. The Prince Regent built a reputation for lavish spending on expensive art and for building large, opulent mansions to house these works.

Young James began his criminal career at around the age of eleven when he stole money from his beloved grandmother, enabling him to see his first show in Drury Lane. He loved the atmosphere and the colour. Theatre became an obsession; one which would require money to purchase tickets.

Soon after attending his first show, he requested money from his grandmother to purchase some new clothes. He used the money to attend the theatre.

He and a couple of mates conspired to steal an expensive fob watch from a well-known gentleman. They were apprehended by the police. James was lucky. The gentleman didn't press charges due to the offenders' age.

James's uncle, who he detested, intervened in the upbringing of the boy when he visited James's grandmother to put forward his plan.

'Moira, I believe we need to do something about James or he'll be swinging from a rope before we know it.'

'I am worried about him, George. He's a good boy at heart. He just got mixed up with the wrong sort.'

'Moira, he needs discipline. I propose he goes to sea; it will build his character.'

'Yes, I agree, although I will miss him terribly.'

James was hauled off by the scruff of the neck to board the brig *Sophia* on which his life at sea was about to begin.

James was bound for Rio de Janeiro on the other side of the world. His uncle had briefed the captain about the trouble James had got himself in with the law. The captain treated the thirteen-year-old as a criminal, meting out punishment for the most trivial offences. The punishment he dreaded most was "mastheading".

Mastheading

James decided he'd had enough of the *Sophia*. He slipped into the Captain's cabin while they were docked at Rio de Janeiro and stole a sizeable amount of money from an unlocked sea chest. He then sailed to Peru on a whaler.

He absconded from the whaler after six months of blood and guts, taking up with a Chilean woman named Catalina.

James had already experienced more life than most, yet he was only sixteen. He was too young to marry the love of his life so he signed up with a

Chilean schooner, the *Liberata*, that transported troops along the Peruvian coast.

James volunteered to fight the Spanish invaders. Chile was fighting a war of independence at that time. The young Englishman survived the war and learned how to fight; James knew he had become a man.

He decided to return to his loved one, Catalina, and marry her.

James, at seventeen, did not understand his marital responsibilities all that well. He and Catalina had two children, a boy and a girl, in the first three years of their marriage. The baby girl lived for only a week. Despite Catalina's devastation, James just took it in his stride.

He became restless. The domestic life didn't suit him and he needed adventure.

He decided to join Thomas Cochrane, the 10th Earl of Dundonald, a captain with a fierce reputation as a naval commander who had never lost a battle. Napoleon called him the *Sea Wolf.*

Having been dismissed from the British Navy for fraud, he became a commander for hire. Brazil, Chile and Peru hired him to rid them of the hated Spanish at an exorbitant fee.

Porter signed up and was soon sailing on a brig heading for Lima. Once docked, he and a couple of shipmates decided to take some unauthorised shore leave and partake in some heavy drinking.

The captain of the brig sent two of his men to drag them back. No doubt, all would be punished.

They found Porter and his mates in a cantina, intoxicated and disorderly. Porter was reluctant to go with the captain's men as were the other two, and a fight broke out.

Porter was proficient with a slingshot. He fired a lead ball at the first mate, hitting him in the back of the head and killing the man.

Porter was now a wanted man. If caught he would hang, but he managed to sign up with a Dutch ship, the *Zierikzee*, heading for England. He behaved himself throughout the voyage and was regarded as a hard- working sailor.

London 1823

James managed to stay away from the law but the temptation to pull off a big job wouldn't go away. He met with two of his good mates from

Bermondsey in a pub called *Hoops and Grapes* in Whitechapel.

'Lads, I've discovered there's a ship moored in the Thames loaded with expensive silks and beaver skins. If we pull off the heist we'll all be rich or at least a lot better off than we all are now,' whispered James.

'Where exactly is she moored, James?' asked Bill Dobson.

'It's off Northfleet.'

Northfleet Dock 1820

That's good. It's a way out of London that'll make it easier to get the booty away.'

The three men slipped aboard the ship, held up the crew guarding it, bound them and seized a significant amount of silks and beaver.

All went well. The three men divided up the spoils and went their separate ways.

Richard Sidebottom was the least intelligent of the three and he began offering silk and beaver to all and sundry, including at his local pub. It didn't take long for the police to hear about it; they arrested him on suspicion. Once they raided his bedsit they secured all the evidence they needed for a conviction.

Unfortunately for Porter and Dobson, Sidebottom spilled the beans, implicating the two and naming Porter as the ringleader.

Porter went before the Bench in Surrey Magistrates Court and after a very brief trial, he was found guilty and sentenced to death.

His sentence was commuted to life of transportation in Van Diemen's Land.

In his first eight months, Porter was imprisoned on a hulk moored in the Thames at Woolwich. Porter, in his diary, wrote that he considered suicide as a viable option.

When he learned of his departure for Van Diemen's Land his spirits lifted. Anything had to be better than the rotten stinking hulk.

The voyage out was uneventful. Porter fitted in with the regime; therefore, he wasn't flogged...unlike some of the other poor bastards. The Roaring Forties was kind to them and the ship arrived in Port Jackson on schedule.

Porter's stay would not be long. His next port of call would be Hobart Town, Van Diemen's Land.

Hobart Town 1820

James scammed his way into the employment of John Pulling, a blacksmith, by stating he had been a beer machine maker in London.

It soon became obvious that he had lied; he didn't know one end of a hammer from the other.

Pulling could have reported Porter to the authorities but he didn't.

Instead, he found him work in the house.

The Pulling household came across hard times and there was barely enough food to put on the table.

Porter was determined to help them through in the only way he knew—thieving.

There were many trading ships moored in the Derwent River. James decided to use the skills learned on the Thames to help the family.

He stole a dinghy and rowed out to the ship he had selected. It was in complete darkness.

He pulled himself up the anchor rope and climbed onto the deck where he crept along until he reached the stairs to the cabins.

He was an experienced thief and he knew where to look. Despite the darkness, he discovered a bag containing three hundred sovereigns as well as some other loose coins.

Once he stuffed his pockets with the booty, he made his way back to the bow of the ship where, to his surprise, he encountered the ship's watchman.

Porter reacted quickly, pushing the bewildered man hard onto the deck. He quickly shimmied down to rope only to find the dinghy had floated off. There was no alternative but to plunge into the icy cold water of the Derwent and swim for shore. He found it difficult, being weighed down by the coins, but he was a strong swimmer.

The alarm had gone out and boats were searching for him but he managed to get ashore.

Proud of his efforts, he returned to the Pullings' house loaded with the silver coins.

'Mrs Pulling, I have a gift for you.'

James pulled the bag out and placed it on the table. He kept the loose coins for himself.

'Oh my God, I don't believe it! Thank you, James, where did you find all this money?'

'Best you don't know, Mrs Pulling.'

'Thank you once again, James, this will save us.'

'It's my pleasure; you and Mr Pulling have been very kind to me.'

When Pulling came into the kitchen having finishing work for the day he couldn't believe his eyes. There were sovereigns spread across the kitchen table.

'Where did all this money come from, Vida?'

'James gave it to us for being kind to him.'

'Vida, how does a convict save this amount of money?'

'I don't know but nevertheless, it will save us from bankruptcy.'

'I'll tell you what… I'm going to turn Mr Porter into the police and they can work out where and how he got it.'

'John, please don't— he was only trying to help.'

'We don't need charity from a convict, Vida. Now that's that; I go to the police tomorrow.

The police did arrest James Porter, but the case was dismissed as nobody could identify the accused.

I'VE GOT TO GET OUT OF THIS PLACE

CHAPTER 2

Governor Arthur was a disciplinarian who would have no hesitation in hanging a convict if he felt it was warranted. He was also a meticulous man who kept detailed records of every convict. His 'black book' recorded every punishment, type of work, character and anything else he felt pertinent to administrating the convict population.

His discipline also applied to the ships moored on the Derwent. If a convict was found on a ship the whole crew would be fined heavily. In some cases, the ship was barred from visiting Hobart Town forever.

May 22 1824

Porter scaled the wall surrounding the Hobart Public Barracks and disappeared for three weeks.

Hobart Public Barracks

Despite the authorities searching, the elusive convict could not be found. It was thought he tried to make it to Bruny Island where he hoped to join a whaler and escape but he told no one of his escapades. After twenty-one days, he was back in his cell in irons, waiting for the inevitable flogging.

'Porter, come with me. The cat's waiting for you,' said Daley, the head gaoler.

Porter had been flogged before so he knew what to expect. He entered the quadrangle where the three sisters stood waiting. Also waiting, holding the cat o' nine tails, was his close friend Dan Glover. It was customary for the prisoner receiving the punishment to be whipped by a friend.

The Three Sisters

The prison guards tied his wrists to the triangle as well as his ankles to bottom posts.

Lieutenant Carew who was now in charge of the guards at the gaol read the order.

'James Porter you have been sentenced to receive one hundred lashes for your crime of absconding from this gaol for three weeks.

'Convict, begin the punishment.'

Convicts chosen to conduct the whipping were usually friends of the convict being flogged. Dan Glover knew if he tried to take it easy on his friend he too would be flogged, and therefore he threw everything into each stroke.

When the 100th lash had struck Porter, his back was red with blood and his backbone could be seen yet throughout the ordeal Porter didn't utter a sound. It wasn't the first time he would feel the cat and nor would it be the last.

Porter was dragged back to his cell. His back looked like mincemeat and his shoes were full of blood. The doctor visited him later in the day and washed the wounds and spread pig's lard all over his back with a cloth.

He was left to reflect on his actions. Was it worth it? Probably not.

When his wounds had healed, he was assigned to the Hobart Town harbourmaster Captain Welsh. He enjoyed his time working with Captain Welsh, who was a fair man who treated his convicts well. Soon young Porter was promoted to coxswain on a six-man rowboat that ferried captains and officials around the harbour.

For the next couple of years, James Porter was a model convict who behaved himself and did not try to escape.

From Scoundrel to Hero

Governor Arthur needed to dispatch an important message to Maria Island, a remote penal colony off the east coast of Van Diemen's Land.

The island was heavily wooded— perfect for harvesting by teams of convicts.

Porter was chosen to head the mission and the authorities even allowed him to choose his own crew.

In good faith, Porter and his crew were provided with firearms and cutlasses for protection against aboriginal attack. The men would have to cross East Bay Neck by foot, carrying the boat. This was an area where the Stony Creek tribe controlled the area and protected it fiercely.

Porter was pleased he had been chosen to lead such an important mission for the governor, despite the arduous trek. He and his crew had to traverse sixty-five miles of land and sea. The route took them from Hobart Town past Sandy Bay, past Bruny Island, heading east and then north. They rounded Lime Bay, continuing on to Norfolk Bay before reaching the narrow neck. It was here where they feared aboriginal attack.

The crew were required to carry the boat once again across the narrow strip of land; this they did without incident until they realised they had been spotted. Spears rained down on Porter and his crew. One man was killed instantly but the rest of the group escaped the attack.

They sailed the seventeen nautical miles to Maria Island, delivering the dispatch.

On their return journey, they were once again attacked but fought back with firearms and cutlasses.

Once they got back to Hobart, they were heralded as heroes. Governor

Arthur awarded them tickets-of-leave.

A tickets-of-leave gives a convict the right to marry and raise a family. They are able to own property and work for wages. However, they cannot carry a firearm or board a ship. They are still convicts but at the top of the pecking order.

Any infringement, no matter how minor, could see the convict lose his privileges.

If a convict tried to escape, he would be demoted from first class to eighth class together with 100 lashes and joining a chain gang: a very slippery slide.

Porter returned to work under his mentor Captain Welsh. He behaved himself apart from the odd indiscretion, which the good captain overlooked.

The lust for freedom never left Porter. He could cope with the arduous work and the floggings but he detested the servitude. He decided it was time to go. He was still intent on making it to Bruny Island and persuading a whaler captain to take him on.

He devised a plan to organise a mass breakout, which should confuse the guards so that they could make their escape. It was not a particularly clever plan, but a plan, nonetheless.

On the night of the breakout, Porter learned that the other convicts were backing out; now it was just him.

Porter was never one to quit so he decided to go it alone. He pushed the guard off the wall and hightailed to the Derwent River with a number of soldiers on his tail. Porter was a very strong swimmer and he knew most of the guards couldn't swim.

Despite the heavy leg irons around his ankles, he made good progress. The soldiers were left on the bank yelling and firing their muskets at nothing in particular, as it was too dark to make out the escaping convict.

Porter avoided the boats that were pursuing him and he doubled back to the shore just behind Government House where Arthur was enjoying a dinner of roast pork and a fine bottle of French wine, totally unaware of the escape.

He struggled to make his way to a friend's house where he thought he might find a safe haven.

Mr Mansfield, a fellow mariner and harbour master, welcomed the wet, bedraggled convict into his home. The kindly man fed Porter and gave him a bed for the night. No mention was made as to why Porter was in ankle chains and no explanation was given.

While lying in bed, Porter devised his next move. He would endeavour to make it to the signal station where he knew his mate would give him shelter. Porter underestimated the power of the pound; Arthur had introduced a scheme whereby a reward of £50 was paid to anyone who could capture an escaped convict.

Porter knocked on the door of the signal station cottage and his mate Luke Carson opened the door.

'James, what are you doing here?'

'I need your help Luke. May I come in?'

'Yes, of course, mate, come in. Can I get you a cup of tea?'

'That would be wonderful, Luke, thank you.'

Luke made a pot of tea and placed some biscuits on a plate.

'There you go, James, get that into you. Now tell me what's going on.'

Porter explained the whole situation from escaping from the gaol until arriving at Luke's door.

'Well, you've done well to make it this far, James, but it's as far as you are going to get.'

Luke grabbed the musket he had placed under the table and pointed it at his so-called friend.

'I'm sorry, Porter, but I'm bringing you in. It's worth £50 which I could really use right now. I lost playing at cards the other night and I'm broke. No hard feelings?'

'You slimy bastard.'

Porter looked around quickly and spotted an axe. He hit Carson across the face, breaking his jaw.

'I have a good mind to finish you off right now.'

Porter left the cottage with Oyster Cove as his intended destination. He knew it would be tough twenty miles of bush and unfamiliar terrain, and he had no compass or provisions. Once there he hoped the lime burners would assist him.

Porter also knew it was a popular spot for escaped convicts and he hoped they would be supportive of him getting across to Bruny Island.

His plan was to steal a boat get to Bruny and hitch up with a whaler. With any luck it would be an American whaler who would take him to Nantucket on the east coast.

Porter spent three days bush bashing through the scrub. He became disoriented and at one stage went around in a complete circle.

He was starving when fortuitously he came across a kangaroo carcass that had been recently killed by what he didn't care. He feasted on the animal and drank its blood. Nourished, he moved on, making the lime burners' camp by the end of the day.

There were two men burning shells left by the aboriginal people and converting it into lime.

'G'day, is it all right to park here for a while?'

'Too right, mate, but where did you come from? You look a right mess.'

'I apologise for the shabby appearance. I've just walked from Hobart Town.'

'With those fucking chains around your ankles; bloody hell mate, you've done well.'

'Aye, I think I have too. Would you two gentlemen consider getting the fucking things off me?'

The two men used the hammers normally used for breaking up the shells to break open the irons.

The next day, Porter went looking for a dinghy to steal to enable him to get to Bruny Island.

He found one beached on the sand with the oars still in it. His luck was still holding until…

A party of soldiers dispatched to find Porter spotted him on the bank and started firing. Porter took to the water, swimming for his life. The pursuing soldiers stopped at the bank since none of them could swim.

James was cold and exhausted. He was halfway to Bruny, but doubted he could go any farther. Then serendipity played its part. A large chunk of kelp drifted past. Porter held onto it and with the incoming tide, he drifted to Bruny Island.

Porter made it shore, wet, shivering and hungry. He knew another convict that resided on the island and this is where he headed for, hoping he would be taken in.

He found the house and knocked on the door. His old mate Henry Forbes answered.

'Well, look what the cat dragged in… James fucking Porter. Come in! You look freezing.'

'Thanks, Henry.'

'First things first. Come and stand in front of the fire. I'll get you some warm clothes.'

Once James changed into the clothes Henry had provided and drank a cup of tea he felt human again.

'So what in the hell have you been up to?' asked Henry.

'I escaped from Hobart Town. I'm hoping to get on a whaler and away from this godforsaken place.'

'How in the hell did you get to Bruny?'

James described his trip with all its trials and tribulations.

'Well mate, you can stay here for a while my governor, Richard Pybuss, is away for a few weeks.'

'Thank you, Henry, that would be excellent. It'll give me time to recuperate from the trek.'

James stayed with Henry for nine days.

On the tenth day, Porter spotted a ship anchored at Esperance Point and he decided this was the opportunity he had hoped for. He attempted to swim out to the vessel but the surf was ferocious. He tried again and again but to no avail.

Mr Pybuss was returning from Hobart Town at the time Porter was attempting to swim through the surf. While in Hobart, the talk of the town was about Porter's escape. Pybuss recognised the escapee and intended to report Porter's presence to the authorities. James, in the meantime, hid in the bush until morning.

The following morning, Porter sighted a boat being rowed with Pybuss up front. He was on his way to report Porter's presence on the island.

Porter decided to try a new approach. He stood up and waved his arms, hoping to attract Pybuss. Pybuss saw him and had the boat turned around and headed for where Porter was standing. He was taken into custody and placed in the bow of the boat.

Porter noticed the boathook, picked it up and threatened Pybuss with it. He demanded to be let off the boat at the bluff.

'Please, if I let you go, the governor will take away my entire convict labour. I'll be ruined,' pleaded Pybuss.

'Well, take me over to that anchored cutter. I'll try my luck with them.'

'Ahoy, may I come aboard?'

'Who are you?'

'James Porter, marooned sailor.'

'Come aboard,' shouted the captain.

Once James was aboard, the captain questioned him and he became convinced Porter was not a marooned sailor but an escaped convict. Porter was arrested but not incarcerated.

One night when no one was looking, he jumped overboard and swam for his life. Porter's luck was still holding.

Porter made his way to Kingston Beach, not far from where he absconded from the clipper. He had another mate who he was sure would put him up. His friend's name was John Brown and he was an ex-convict.

As it turned out the loyal and trusted friend was a turncoat. Just as James had settled in, there was a loud knock on the door. Brown opened it and six soldiers stormed in and arrested James Porter. The £50 reward would come in handy.

January 30 1830

Porter's trial lasted only an hour and he was found guilty of being "illegally at large while under a second conviction".

He was sentenced to hang.

LIFE ON SARAH ISLAND

CHAPTER 3

James Porter was in an environment he knew well; a dark, damp, putrid cell waiting for the guard to escort him to the gallows.

He was unaware that his mentor Captain Welsh was pleading for his life, giving the magistrate a glowing character reference. The young man's record over the previous four years did not support Captain Welsh's words.

Porter was escorted back to court to hear the good news— or was it?

Captain Welsh was successful in persuading the magistrate to commute James Porter's sentence to seven years hard labour in hell; Sarah Island, Macquarie Harbour.

Porter was sent back to his cell awaiting transportation to Sarah Island.

A week later, two guards entered his cell and fitted him with new and much heavier chains. They then manhandled him out to take him to the wharf. He had a new uniform. It was labelled the 'harlequin uniform', and was made up of yellow and black patches. The yellow was the colour of disgrace; men who wore it were called 'canary men'. Porter knew this was the start of humiliation and hard labour. He hoped he could last the seven years without being broken.

Porter was marched down to the dock along with several other unfortunates and boarded the *Prince Leopold*.

Porter said his farewells to Hobart Town; a place he had grown fond of despite his detention. He knew all the privileges he had enjoyed, including the odd glass of beer and tea and biscuits, were gone.

The convicts, including Porter, were located in the ship's hold. It was going to be a very uncomfortable journey and their irons remained on for the entire time.

James was reasonably lucky. The time to sail from Hobart Town to Macquarie Harbour took a little over two weeks but some poor wretches were in the hold for three months.

The *Prince Leopold* waited outside of the harbour until a pilot arrived to guide them through the treacherous entrance aptly named 'Devil's Gates'.

Devil's Gates

Macquarie Harbour was vast. It looked as if the water was poisoned as it had a red-brown tinge to it. It was, however, perfectly clean with an abundance of fish. The colour came from the Gordon River, which was rich in tannins.

Macquarie Harbour

The harbour was surrounded by temperate rainforest and wooded mountains. This terrain made it very difficult for convicts to escape.

The *Price Leopold* sailed slowly up to the far end of the harbour where

Sarah Island was located.

Sarah Island

The *Prince Leopold* dropped anchor close to the island. Boats rowed out to collect the arrivals and take them to their new home.

Porter could see stone quarters he assumed would be his new domicile. There were also soldiers' barracks, what looked like a penitentiary, and a number of other dwellings.

Porter stepped onto the island with great trepidation. The stories of Sarah Island instilled fear in all the convicts in Van Diemen's Land.

Two guards grabbed Porter and marched him up to the commandant's office. Captain James Briggs was not a man who was known for his kindness, but rather for his ruthlessness.

Captain Briggs addressed the man in the harlequin uniform standing before him.

'Porter, I know of your reputation and have read your record. I can assure you there is no means of escape from Sarah Island. If you work hard and obey orders your time here will be tolerable. If you misbehave, it will become intolerable.

'You will be housed on Grummet Island initially until you prove yourself worthy. That is all.'

Map 4. Sarah Island Settlement 1824

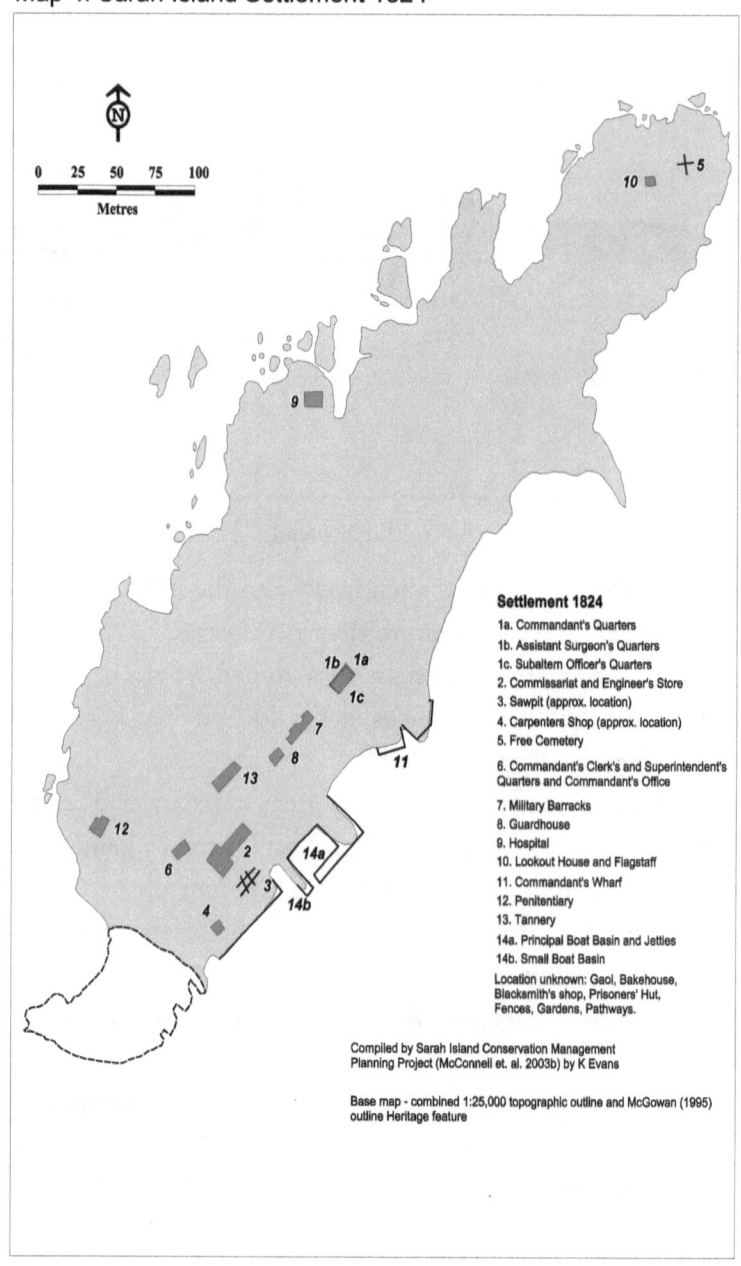

0   25   50   75   100

Metres

Settlement 1824

1a. Commandant's Quarters
1b. Assistant Surgeon's Quarters
1c. Subaltern Officer's Quarters
2. Commissariat and Engineer's Store
3. Sawpit (approx. location)
4. Carpenters Shop (approx. location)
5. Free Cemetery
6. Commandant's Clerk's and Superintendent's Quarters and Commandant's Office
7. Military Barracks
8. Guardhouse
9. Hospital
10. Lookout House and Flagstaff
11. Commandant's Wharf
12. Penitentiary
13. Tannery
14a. Principal Boat Basin and Jetties
14b. Small Boat Basin

Location unknown: Gaol, Bakehouse, Blacksmith's shop, Prisoners' Hut, Fences, Gardens, Pathways.

Compiled by Sarah Island Conservation Management Planning Project (McConnell et. al. 2003b) by K Evans

Base map - combined 1:25,000 topographic outline and McGowan (1995) outline Heritage feature

Convicts towing a raft of Huon pine logs. Sketch by Thomas Lempriere c.1829.

Grummet Island

Grummet Island was about two hundred metres north of Sarah Island. It was a small island; no more than a rocky outcrop covered in bush.

At its highest point was a building with four small rooms where the most hardened convicts would sleep in very cramped conditions. They slept in their uniforms, which were more often than not soaking wet from the day's work of pulling Huon pine logs out to the transfer boats.

Heating came from a wood heater, which was difficult to light and difficult to keep going, as the wood they were given was green. Captain Briggs did not want the convicts to have dry wood which would float and therefore, tempt the convicts to build a raft.

Porter's day began with a weak porridge that was difficult to digest unless you were starving which Porter and the others invariably were. They needed some nourishment to cope with the arduous day ahead.

Once breakfast was consumed, a boat took the convicts over to Sarah Island where they cut down large Huon pines with axes and saws.

The logs were then dragged down to the boat builders to be used in constructing brigs and other vessels. The Huon pine is a soft wood known for its oiliness, which makes it malleable and easy to work with. It is also extremely waterproof, making it perfect for shipbuilding.

The work was gruelling, but to make it even worse they were in chains.

After a twelve-hour day, the convicts were taken back to Grummet Island.

As they hadn't eaten since breakfast, they were starving. They then had to cook their own supper from meagre provisions that were often spoiled.

After a fitful sleep, the whole procedure began again. No wonder convicts committed suicide or in some cases committed murder so they could be hanged with a priest's blessing to ensure their place in heaven.

Porter seriously considered taking his own life, but the thought of escape prevented him. Where there was hope there was life.

The prisoners were punished for the smallest of infringements the most common form of punishment was "the Macquarie cat".

The Macquarie Harbour cat o' nine tails was reputed to be heavier and larger than that of the army or navy. It had seven knots in each tail and a double twisted whipcord rather than the usual single cord.

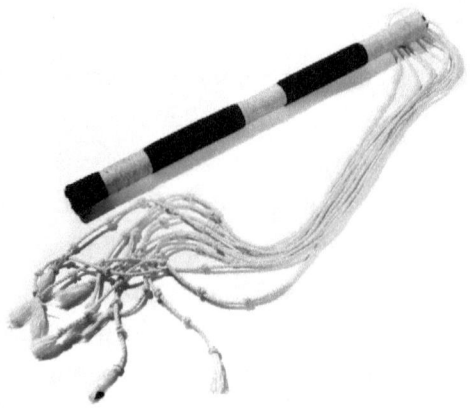

Particularly during the early years of the penal settlement, the formidable 'Macquarie cat' was used with relentless frequency. In the first seven years of the settlement, an average of 6560 lashes per year was inflicted on 175 men. However, in the last five years of the settlement, when Porter was on the island, this had dropped dramatically to an average of 850 lashes per year inflicted on 25 men.

Porter had endured twelve months on Grummet Island when he learned that he would be transferred to the main island. This news didn't bring joy to the hardened convict, yet he knew it had to be better than living on the small island. His thoughts centred on escape.

The day began in the usual way. The sun rose and the convicts ate their gruel. Each man was checked for contraband and boarded the launch, which would take the seventeen convicts to a timber camp at Kelly Basin at the far eastern end of Macquarie Harbour.

As they approached the shore, Porter looked at James Sheedy and William Holt. A slight nod of the head indicated to Porter all was well.

A few yards from the shore, the three men jumped up, brandishing axes that been hidden from view. The two soldiers on board had no idea what was happening and before they knew it the renegade convicts were threatening them with their weapons. They just sat there aghast at what was happening. Porter's men grabbed their muskets and instructed them to sit in the bottom of the boat with their hands on their heads.

The rest of the convicts in the boat looked on in both amazement and amusement. It wasn't very often they had such entertainment. Having heard it said that these three convicts were very dangerous; they would not do anything to upset them.

Once Porter was sure all seventeen occupants were under control, he jumped out and waded through twelve inches of Macquarie Harbour. He called on Sheedy to pass him the muskets. Holt ensured all the oars were collected and piled on the beach.

The three escapees gave the boat a huge shove out into the harbour. It drifted out thirty yards and was then becalmed. All the passengers just looked at each other in bewilderment as none of them could swim.

Porter, Sheedy and Holt headed off to climb Sugarloaf Mountain, to view the harbour traffic and the surrounding terrain and plot their escape.

Porter was confident that with the seventeen drifting aimlessly, it would be some time before they were pursued.

The three escapees made the difficult ascent of Sugarloaf Mountain, which took them the best part of the day. They sat on a large rock surveying the harbour and what they saw dismayed them. A detachment of soldiers was rescuing their comrades and the Grummet Island convicts. They looked over to Sarah Island where smoke was billowing skywards signalling *man on the run*.

'Come on, we've got to move quickly. The bastards will have soldiers posted at every exit,' said Porter.

'We can't be on the run without food. If we have empty bellies we'll just collapse and wait to be captured,' said Sheedy.

'I know, my plan is to head for the sawyers' camp at Phillip's Creek and steal as much food as we can carry.'

That was the plan and they executed it skilfully. They stole food from all the sawyers' tents… enough to keep them going for days.

They hid the food by burying it on the beach wrapped in cloth to be retrieved when they secured a boat.

'That's the first part of the plan achieved. Now we need to steal a boat,' said Porter.

'Easier said than done, Porter. Where are we going to find one?' said Holt.

'On Phillip Island. It's not that far to swim and there are plenty of boats over there.'

Fortunately, all three men could swim and once on the island they found a suitable craft. As they were dragging it to the water's edge, they heard a loud voice.

'What the fuck do you think you're doing, you fucking thieves? That's my dinghy.'

'Not anymore it's not; we need it more than you— now bugger off.'

'I'm not letting you take it and that's that.'

'There's three of us and we're on the run from Briggs. If you don't get out of the way we'll beat you to a pulp. The good news is when we row as far as we can up the Gordon we'll leave the boat on the shore. It should be easy to find,' said Porter.

The man saw their point of view and let them take the boat.

The search for the escapees was on; soldiers had been posted all around the area with orders; shoot to kill.

The three convicts lay low among the rushes observing the frantic activity.

Porter's conundrum was how to recover the food packages, for without them, they were doomed.

'Listen up, men. I think the only way we can recover the food parcels is to row over after dark when with any luck they won't spot us.'

They rowed over to the beach, dug up the parcels and began rowing up river unseen by those who were searching for them.

The Gordon River is slow moving. Its colour resembled strong tea and its other feature is that it has many bends which makes it difficult to see what's ahead.

As the three escapees hugged the shore to escape a fast-moving current, a large boat manned with soldiers spotted them. Porter, Sheedy and Holt rowed like the devil heading for the shore. The larger boat had four oarsmen and was gaining on the dinghy fast. The convicts made it to shore before being apprehended and ran into the rainforest. They had to leave their food parcel behind. They weren't dressed for scrambling through the thick rainforest. Fallen trees, barbed vines and thick scrub made their progress very slow.

Everything was wet. Their clothes became drenched.

They had been in the rainforest for two torturous days but it seemed like twenty. They slept on the damp forest floor and there was nothing available to keep them warm.

When Porter and his mates had been on the run for four days, they were woken by the blast of a rifle. They looked up only to see a group of soldiers all with their rifles pointed at them.

Porter recognised a convict by the name of John Little. It was he who had found his fellow convicts. He would have received a sizeable reward.

Porter and the other men were almost thankful for being found as they all knew they wouldn't have lasted another day.

The men all needed assistance to be able to walk back to the penal settlement. They were placed in cold dark cells until their punishment of one hundred lashes with the Macquarie cat was administered.

Back in their cells, leg irons were attached to their ankles. These would remain for the next six months as part of their punishment.

THERE'S A NEW SHERIFF IN TOWN

CHAPTER 4

A new commandant had arrived on the island to replace Briggs, his name was Major Pery Baylee, a much more compassionate man than his predecessor.

'Captain Briggs, don't you think the punishment for these men is rather harsh? You saw the condition they were in when they were brought back in. What they endured in the bush was punishment in itself.'

'Major Baylee, you have hardly set foot on Sarah Island and you are giving me instruction as to how I manage my convicts. I would ask you to keep your opinions to yourself until I leave the island.

'I am still Commandant and as such I order you to witness the floggings at 7 am tomorrow.'

'Yes, sir, but I will make my objection known to Governor Arthur.'

'You can do what you like.'

At 6.55 am the three escaped convicts were led out from their cells and tied to the whipping triangles.

At 7 am convicts known to them made the first stroke.

By 8 am they were all back in their cells bleeding profusely and semi-conscious.

Major Baylee nearly fainted, but held firm.

When Captain Briggs left Sarah Island in 1832, everybody on the island, including the soldiers and their officers, were pleased to see him go.

The atmosphere on Sarah Island changed as soon as Briggs departed. Baylee used the lash and the solitary confinement cells infrequently. He was known to walk among the convicts without a guard chatting to the prisoners.

Baylee closed the infamous Grummet Island. The convicts were eating nutritious food; he built a new three-storey penitentiary with proper heating and a comfortable space to sleep.

Also under his tenure, a school thrived, teaching convicts to read and write as well as basic mathematics.

Instead of the dreary morose prison island, Sarah Island became a much happier place. It was a hive of activity with convicts producing fine furniture, panel doors, and windows all out of Huon pine. Even buckets and wheelbarrows and oars were produced.

The mainstay was still shipbuilding. Several brigs had been built at the Sarah Island shipyard, including the infamous *Cyprus*. The shipbuilding was managed by David Hoy, a master shipwright regarded as one of the most gifted shipbuilders in the modern world.

The convicts that worked under his direction admired him and he was the most respected officer in the colony.

Hoy's attitude was 'work hard for me and you will be rewarded with new skills.' He also allowed his men to make objects for sale on the side. As long as this activity didn't impact the work on the ships he was quite willing to turn a blind eye.

Convicts began making a variety of things from polished walking sticks to garments. The illicit trade flourished and convicts could now get their hands on tobacco and rum.

Apart from building brigs, the shipyards produced schooners, sloops, cutters and launches. A total of 130 ships were built under Hoy's management.

In the latter part of 1832, Governor Arthur declared that Sarah Island would be closing down and the newly constructed Port Arthur would become the new penal settlement. Located on the Tasman Peninsula, Port Arthur was a much larger establishment than Macquarie Harbour. Arthur built the penal settlement so that he could consolidate the worst of the worst convicts.

Port Arthur could house 1100 convicts; twice as many as Sarah Island, and all held within a confined space. This made it easier to control the prison population.

Port Arthur grew from humble beginnings as a logging camp into a successful commercial enterprise, which paid its way.

PORT ARTHUR, DURING OCCUPATION A.D 1860. 214. BEATTIE, HOBART

The evacuation of Sarah Island was not quick. It took from January 1833 until October 1834 when the *Charlotte* and the *Tamar* transported the last of the convicts to Port Arthur. That left only a handful of convicts, including Porter, to finish the half-built brig the *Frederick*.

Arthur wanted the brig to be disassembled and reassembled at Port Arthur, but Hoy insisted the *Frederick* must be seaworthy before sailing to the new penal establishment.

Hoy handpicked the men he wanted to complete the build; Porter was one of the chosen few. For the previous few months, he had acted as pilot boat's coxswain, away from the timber cutting and using his maritime skills.

The government in Hobart decided that a combination of sailors and mechanics were required to complete the *Frederick's* build. Four soldiers would be responsible for guarding the workforce.

The harbour master, Charles Taw, would be Hoy's deputy.

Charles Lyon and James Leslie, experienced mariners, were selected to be part of the crew who would sail the completed brig to its new home at Port Arthur.

Taw would be captain and a free man, James Tate, would be his first mate.

The balance of the crew would be selected from the remaining convicts on Sarah Island. The crewmen were:

John Barker; aged 37.

Barker was the most senior of the convicts in the construction team. Barker's trade in England was gunsmith and watchmaker. Hoy saw Barker as the foreman of the group He relied heavily on Barker during the construction of the *Fredrick*.

As with most of the convicts, a single indiscretion saw him transported to Bermuda where all the convicts were housed in stinking decaying hulks and forced to break up limestone to construct a large breakwater.

He was then transferred to Australia where his record became black. His initial sentence was seven years, but after receiving a stolen watch it doubled to fourteen. He then did a runner from a chain gang, and when captured, he was sentenced to life at Macquarie Harbour.

He spent an inordinate amount of time with a fellow convict; William Phillips, who was proficient in navigation particularly 'dead reckoning' commonly known as navigation by the stars. He became proficient himself.

Charles Lyon; aged 28

Lyon was Scottish, from Dundee and he was transported to Australia on the same ship as Porter. He too had gone to sea at a very early age. He was convicted of breaking and entering at eighteen and sentenced to transportation.

From a very quiet passive young man, captivity transformed him into an aggressive malicious individual.

His transgressions included drunkenness on many occasions, beating and assaulting his master's servant, idleness and neglect of duty. He was accused of highway robbery but the case was dismissed. The final straw was when he was convicted of rape; for this, he was sentenced to hang. The sentence was commuted to life at Macquarie Harbour.

Porter and Barker regarded Lyon as a very dangerous man.

James Leslie; aged 25

Leslie was the opposite of Lyon. He was a gentle likeable man who liked to abscond just as Porter did. He was a shipwright, and therefore, an invaluable member of the team.

He was transported for stealing and once in the colony he committed several transgressions but nothing serious. The most common offence was being absent without leave.

John Jones; aged 42

The elder of the group, he had only arrived in Australia a few months before being transferred to Sarah Island for the express purpose of being part of the crew to sail the *Frederick* back to Port Arthur.

He was a Bermuda veteran like Barker and he had received several sentence extensions over a long and illustrious criminal career.

John Fare; aged 27

Fare had been convicted of housebreaking and was serving a seven-year sentence. He had only one charge against his name since arriving in Australia and that was for drunkenness.

John Dady; aged 23

Dady was a part of the carpentry team, therefore, a critical spoke in the wheel. He was transported for stealing a handkerchief. By committing various offences he spent a significant amount of time in chains or on the dreaded treadmill.

The visiting French naval officer Hyacinthe de Bougainville gave this account of the Sydney treadmill in 1825:

It is a large wheel whose horizontal blades are wide enough to allow a certain number of men to position themselves, each next to the other, on the outside...Holding on to a wooden crossbar that is separate from the wheel and attached at the height of the chin, they climb without stopping from one blade to the next...this labour continues for forty minutes without a break; the men rest for twenty minutes, then they start up again, and so on, for the whole day...It was difficult to imagine an activity more boring and tiring at the same time, by its monotony and the care necessary to apply to this task, in the fear of missing the blade and having your legs mutilated...

Dady must have had a fetish for clothes as one time he was caught with a frock and a pair of stockings and received fifty lashes. Another time he was caught with two pairs of trousers.

Billy Shires; aged 39

Billy was the longest serving convict of the group, yet he had the cleanest sheet. Convicted of highway robbery in England, he was transported for life. He leaned his carpentry skills while in captivity. By the time he joined the shipbuilding crew he had served thirteen years.

Benjamin Russen; aged 30

Ben had been convicted of burglary in Norwich, before arriving in Australia in 1822. Like Porter and Leslie, he was a bolter and received many lashes as a result. It seemed as though Ben would be flogged for the slightest indiscretion such as twenty-five lashes for not paying attention.

William Cheshire; aged 24

At four feet eleven, William was regarded as a runt. He'd been a butcher in Birmingham when he decided to break into a house.

He was part of the team because he was Barker's servant. He did have carpentry skills and experience, but he was not highly regarded.

What a bunch of misfits, all hardened criminals apart from two!

Hoy and Taw were confident that these men would build the ship to the highest standard.

WE ARE PIRATES

CHAPTER 5

The date to sail the *Frederick* out of Hell's Gates had been chosen; weather permitting, as the 25th of January. The crew who would sail her were finalising the preparations for the journey except for Cheshire who did nothing.

Porter had no time for little runt; he had contributed very little to the building. In fact, he got in the way more than anything.

As the launch date was drawing close the convict crew were finalising their plan to seize the brig and sail off into the Pacific just as Swallow had done in the *Cyprus*.

The conspirators could talk to each other quite freely. After all, they were trusted members of the team. That was not to say discretion at all times was not required.

Two of the future pirates, Leslie and Russen, let their guard slip. They were discussing the plan in their cabin unaware that Cheshire was listening at the door. The little weasel ran back to inform his master Barker of the conspiracy.

Barker called for a secret meeting with the nine convicts who were still part of the plan to seize the brig.

'We have a traitor among us. It's the runt Cheshire. From now on, don't trust the bastard.'

'What are we going to do about the snitch?' asked Leslie.

'In my opinion, there are only two alternatives; slit his throat or invite him in. The former would ruin our plans as the authorities would not look kindly on a murder, particularly during the last days of the island,' said Porter.

'Right, well, I'll have a chat with him and invite him to join us. Having said that we need to keep a very close eye on him,' said Barker.

By early January all was well for the escape. There was to be a launch and trial, testing all aspects of the newly completed ship on January 12. Although the *Frederick* was on a trial, all the provisions needed for the voyage had been already loaded.

As the *Frederick* slid down the runway and into Macquarie Harbour, a light south-westerly was blowing.

Taw made for the treacherous Hell's Gates.

By mid-afternoon, the wind had turned to north-westerly and was blowing strongly, making the swell at Hell's Gates dangerously high. Taw decided to anchor on the lee side of Wellington Head and wait for more favourable winds. His hope was for conditions to improve on the morrow so they could continue their journey.

The delay suited the mutineers as it gave them more time to plan the seizure of the ship.

Barker went below to where he had a cache of weapons he had forged while on the island. He had fashioned pistols out of old muskets and he had also forged tomahawks, all razor sharp. The mutineers would be well armed and a match for the four soldiers aboard.

Captain Taw was disappointed the following day which was just as inclement as the previous one. Porter and Barker took advantage. They suggested to two of the soldiers that some fishing was in order and they both agreed.

Later in the day, the soldiers were ready to go with the fishing tackle in hand. Captain Taw's servant James Macfarlane had decided to join them, along with Porter. They lowered the jolly boat, which was normally used to ferry passengers to and from shore.

Porter excused himself, indicating he was not well, and the fishing party of three took off, hopeful of catching some fish for their supper.

Porter turned to Barker with a sly grin.

'And then there were two.'

Captain Taw and the shipwright Hoy were in the captain's cabin drinking before enjoying a dinner prepared by Nichols, the captain's servant.

Knowing this, Porter suggested to one of the soldiers, a young corporal, that they too deserved a tot of rum. They both went below in good spirits.

Barker invited the other soldier to join them but he wasn't interested. He would stay at his post, ever vigilant.

Russen and Leslie slowly moved into position. Russen was behind the windlass, the crane used to haul heavy objects aboard, while Leslie pretended to be working at something or another.

A signal was given and the two mutineers ran for the soldier and held him down. In the meantime, Barker and Fare were also back on deck and became involved, holding their axes close to the petrified soldier's neck. He just lay there, realising it was folly to resist. Barker gagged him and tied his feet and hands.

Shires had been itching for a fight since being locked up by Captain Taw for insubordination. He heard the commotion on the deck and he looked over at the corporal, who was finishing his second rum. He leaped at the unsuspecting soldier, hitting him in the head with a clenched fist. The other convicts pinned him down.

'Move and I'll kill you,' said Shires, holding an axe above his head.

'Put them the forecastle and make sure they're secure,' said Porter.

'We'd better grab Tate. I think he's in his cabin,' said Barker.

Russen called out to the first mate to come up on deck.

When Tate arrived, Russen grabbed him and threatened him with a tomahawk. Jones and Lyon assisted Russen. They tied the first mate's hands and gagged him before throwing him into the forecastle with the two soldiers.

'The jolly boat will be back soon with the other two soldiers. We need to take care of Taw and Hoy before they return,' said Barker.

'You're right; let's go,' said Porter.

All ten convicts were aware that if any of their hostages were harmed in any way they would all be hanged if they were caught. There was none more vigilant about not harming their captives than Shires.

Porter and Shires began their descent to the aft of the ship where the captain's quarters were located. Porter asked Shires to wait while he diverted to collect the remaining weapons and ammunition in steerage.

Shires could hear raucous laughter coming from the captain's cabin.

They're pissed on our rum ration no doubt, he thought.

He decided not to wait for Porter. He opened the hatch and jumped in, bypassing the stairs altogether.

Hoy and Taw were in total shock. There was Shires threatening them with an axe.

'Give yourselves up. We have the ship.'

Porter returned from collecting the guns only to find Shires had started without him. The two men were putting up an admirable fight and Shires was struggling. As Captain Taw tried to constrain Shires, the convict hit him with the axe. Hoy attempted to come to his friend's aid but was rebuffed by the much stronger, much younger, Shires.

Shires began to realise that both men, being drunk, had acquired some Dutch courage. It became all too much for the convict and he scampered up the stairs, through the hatch, into the bosom of his mates who were looking on.

'Come on out, we will not harm you,' Barker yelled.

'We will not yield,' replied Taw.

Porter knew there were pistols and muskets located in the captain's quarters. By their tone of voice, they were intending to put up a good fight. He was conscious of the fact that if the two men were injured or, God forbid, killed, they would all hang.

A stalemate developed with Taw and Hoy holding loaded pistols and the convicts unwilling to enter the cabin.

Porter and Barker were becoming anxious. The jolly boat would be returning from the fishing expedition shortly, and they needed the stalemate to end.

Porter and Barker conferred. They decided to point a couple of muskets down through the hatch, being careful not to hit anyone. It was a bluff more than anything.

One of the musket's ball shots hit a bunch of keys Taw was holding. They were shot out of his hand, but luckily, Taw was not injured.

It had the desired effect and both men surrendered to the convicts.

'I assume you will not injure us.'

'I give you my word,' yelled Porter.

The two men, looking dishevelled and ashen-faced, climbed up the stairs to be met by the convicts they had trusted throughout the building of the *Fredrick*.

Hoy came up first. He was greeted with two convicts aiming muskets at his chest. His hands were bound and he was led off.

Taw was reluctant to follow but eventually did so. He too had his hands bound and was led off. The wound on his forehead could be seen clearly.

Finally, Nicholls, Taw's servant, emerged. He had remained hidden during the entire fracas.

Once all three were locked safely away in the forecastle, Porter turned his attention to the jolly boat and the two soldiers returning soon.

Porter chose John Fare to fire a shot close to the boat. He then signalled for them to return to the ship post haste, which they did.

As they reached the *Frederick,* Porter jumped aboard holding a musket cocked and ready to fire at the stunned men.

Within a short time, both soldiers were relieved of their weapons and brought on board to be contained with the other captives.

The *Frederick* had new owners. It had taken only a few hours and nobody was seriously hurt.

Hoy asked who would be captain from now on.

'That would be me, Mr Hoy,' said John Barker.

'And you think you can sail her off into the blue yonder?'

'I do, with the help of Mr Porter and my men.'

'You are deluded. I promise before God and a bible in my hand that if you give us back the brig, nobody will mention what happened today when we reach Port Arthur.'

'We will not yield the ship. All we want is our liberty,' Barker replied.

The thought of Port Arthur and what awaited them when they arrived was the reason for seizing the *Frederick* in the first place.

WE ARE SAILING

CHAPTER 6

Hoy and Taw were escorted below deck to their cabins and permitted to take anything they thought was required. Warm attire was the priority, as Macquarie Harbour became cold at night even in summer.

Like the castaways from the *Cyprus* it was clear the group would have to find their way back to Hobart Town.

Once packed, the two men were escorted to the main deck to be joined by the others.

'Mr Hoy, please accept this bottle of rum and this compass. I think you will need both,' said Shires.

'Thank you Shires, but don't believe I will be forgiving you for what you did to Captain Taw.'

'I understand, sir.'

It was time to go. Hoy and Taw were the first to be lowered into the jolly boat, then the first mate and then the four soldiers were lowered down. Finally, two convicts who were not part of the plot were lowered.

Behind them, was the longboat with six armed convicts who would trail them to the shore.

Before they all got underway Barker yelled his final instruction to Hoy.

'When you reach the shore push the boat out and the whaleboat will tow her back.'

'I was hoping we could keep it. We might have a better chance of getting back to Hobart Town by sea.'

'I'm sorry, but we can't risk you coming back and rushing the ship tonight.'

There was no frivolity on the *Frederick* that night. The convicts kept a strict watch. Barker made it very clear that if anyone on watch fell asleep they would be put to death.

When the sun rose, Porter led a group of convicts to where the castaways were huddled behind some bushes close to the sand.

Hoy had requested bandages and plaster for his back. The convicts also gave him two bottles of wine to help ease the pain.

The four soldiers were given back their thick woollen watch coats.

The next task was to divide the *Frederick's* provisions; unlike what happened to the *Cyprus* survivors the convicts split the entire provisions down the middle. There would be no starvation in this group.

The provisions consisted of flour, oatmeal, and salted beef as well as tea, biscuits and sugar.

Finally, a goat that Shires had named Lucy was handed over, along with cooking utensils.

All the convicts, particularly Shires, were conscious of the inhumane way the *Cyprus* castaways were treated and they were determined their castaways would be treated fairly.

Once the distribution of food was completed, Hoy made a final plea that they should return the ship. The convicts politely declined. Hoy then gave them what only could be considered his blessing.

'Since I find you will not give her up, I thank you all for your kindness to the whole of us and myself in particular. I know you have but little provisions to cross the expanding ocean and likewise a brig that is not seaworthy for such a voyage and may God prosper you in all your perilous undertaking.'

The other castaways all wished the convicts plain sailing and a prosperous voyage.

Captain Taw was the one with most to lose. He had lost his ship and he knew he would never get another one.

January 13 1833

The convict crew of the *Frederick* all stared back at the shore. They waved at the castaways and Hoy, Taw and the other men waved back. There was surprisingly no animosity between the two groups.

As the *Frederick* made her way heading for Hell's Gates, the convicts felt for the first time in a very long time; true freedom.

Porter, Leslie, Russen and Lyon had all been in custody for more than ten years, and Shires for fourteen. The two least experienced convicts were Jones and Fare, who had arrived in Van Diemen's Land in July 1832.

Barker, the ringleader, had been in the colony six years but he was serving a life sentence.

Barker and Porter felt comfortable that they had a head start on any ship sent to pursue them.

They knew it would take several weeks before the authorities in Hobart would be alerted that the *Frederick* had not arrived at Port Arthur. A search party would need to be assembled and this would take time; possibly three days. A crew would need to be called for duty and that also could take some time.

The two men deduced that with favourable winds the *Frederick* should be far away by the time their pursuers set sail; after all, they would have been sailing for a month.

Captain Barker skilfully manoeuvred the *Frederick* through Hell's Gates, a treacherous passage where many ships had foundered.

Porter stood on the deck with a sense of euphoria overwhelming him. He could not remember being so happy.

The *Frederick*

'Porter, we need to make her as light as possible. We will need to outrun the British warship they are no doubt sending to capture us. Please organise the men to break up the whale boat and discard her pieces overboard. She

170

weighs seven tons. I should know— I built her.'

'Is that wise, Captain? You never know when we might need her what with the jolly boat gone.'

'I can assure you, Porter, she is more use to us broken up and over the side. Get on with it.'

'Yes, Captain.'

The *Frederick* was now without a longboat if they needed her.

The wind had strengthened and by the next morning the brig was powering through the ocean at twelve knots, which was quite a reasonable speed for a ship the size of the *Frederick*. Barker was aware that too much sail could be dangerous, and therefore he set a very conservative sail.

They were heading on a west-south-west course away from Van Diemen's Land, hoping to avoid any shipping in the area.

As the *Frederick* sailed through the blue ocean water, the crew were ecstatic. The wind was in their faces and they were free men at last. What could be better?'

Barker and Porter were below deck and Shires was at the wheel. The two senior men were checking the charts and discussing where they should be heading to be out of harm's way.

'We seem to be making good headway, Barker. The ship is performing admirably,' said Porter.

'Yes, it's not the ship that concerns me, Porter, although she wasn't built for the open sea as you know... she was built for the coast. We have a crew of which half are untrained and inexperienced. When we encounter a storm, and we will, we could be in deep trouble.'

'We do have five experienced sailors aboard. The others will just have to learn the ropes from them.'

'I suppose so.'

Just like the *Cyprus* and other pirate ships, every crewmember on the *Frederick* would get a vote. If the crew outvoted the captain he was obliged to accept the majority vote.

The first vote for the Sarah Island convicts would determine what part of the world they would sail to.

Barker called the crew together in the mess to make this critical decision.

'Right, men, we need to make the decision about where we will head. If we don't make it now we will be sailing around aimlessly waiting for a British warship to intercept us. Does anybody here have any suggestions?'

'How about Tahiti?' suggested Charles Lyon.

'We know from *Cyprus*'s experience that the natives of Tahiti no longer wish to have British sailors there. Apparently, they can be quite aggressive. The other issue is that British warships visit the area regularly, primarily to track down escaped convicts,' said Barker.

'I vote for Tonga. Swallow spoke highly of the place,' said John Fare.

'Your vote is noted, John. The only problem I see with Tonga is that the British warships visit regularly.'

'I vote for America,' said Ben Russen.

'I vote for Chile,' said James Porter.

'Why Chile, James?' asked John Jones.

'It's the last place the British Navy will look for us, it has a great climate and the women are very accommodating.'

'I agree with Porter. Chile is our safest option,' said Barker.

Barker asked for a show of hands. Chile won six to four.

CHILE

CHAPTER 7

There were advantages in choosing Chile. They would be sailing with the prevailing winds, making the journey relatively fast. The other advantage was they would not be sailing near the busy shipping lanes, giving them anonymity.

Chile had fought and won a war of independence against Spain. They also had no allegiance to Britain and the country was completely independent. This fact gave the pirates hope that they would be accepted as refugees and not escaped convicts. Their ambition was to be allowed to settle in Chile.

Barker and Porter had their reservations about the crossing; the *Frederick* was a small ship; 130 tons in all, where the cargo ships crossing the Pacific from Australia to Chile were up to 300 tons and built for heavy seas, not speed.

A more pressing issue had presented itself. Only one of the two pumps was working and this would require the working pump to be operated constantly. It would be hard on the crew as the pumps took enormous strength to operate efficiently.

The favourable winds that took the *Frederick* out of Macquarie Harbour and on its way to Chile were now becoming stronger. The little brig was sailing beautifully, however, the wind kept getting stronger and stronger and they were now sailing in a gale.

The waves were breaking over the deck and inexperienced crew members were terrified now the *Frederick* was rising and falling thirty feet. Lyon was at the helm struggling with the wheel yet keeping the brig on course.

The *Frederick* was groaning under the strain, her green timbers threatening to crack. Waves were smashing into the bow, spraying freezing water over the deck and crew.

Lyon was exhausted. He was wet through, his arms ached and he needed support but none came. The rest of the crew were busy with the sails.

The sails looked likely to blow out and they needed to be lowered as quickly as possible.

Fare was in charge of the sails as he had the experience as a foremast man on several ships. He shouted that he needed six men to bring down as many sails as they could. They were successful, and although John Dady slipped while at the top of the mast, he was able to grab a sail as he was plummeting down to the deck and certain death.

If the sails had remained up the chance of the mast snapping was great.

Every man was soaking and exhausted but they had to keep going. The storm was unrelenting the sails that remained were soaked, even the fore-royal.

It was a vision of chaos with men sliding along the deck bumping into others who were trying to get back to their post. Ropes and deck fittings became the crew's lifeline.

Fare instructed four crew to climb up and take down the main topsail, which looked about to tear. They achieved this task despite the severe roll of the ship.

The gale wasn't abating, in fact, it seemed to be getting more severe. Lyon was at the point of exhaustion. He needed another man to assist him at the wheel. Porter instructed one of the men on the pump to come up on deck and assist the exhausted helmsman.

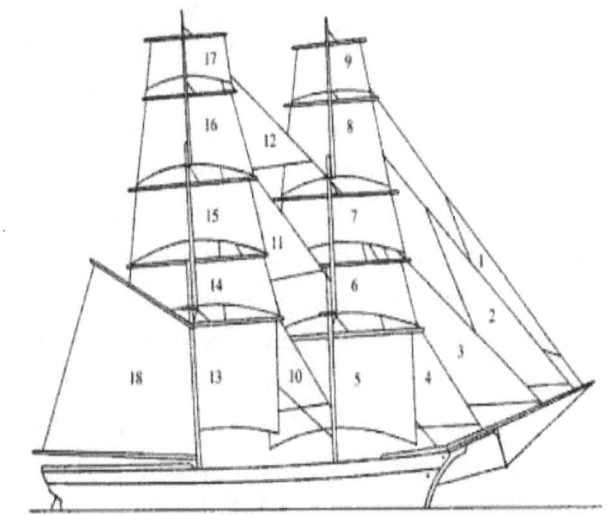

Brig

1 Middle staysail (flying jib)
2 Outer jib
3 Inner jib
4 Fore-topmast staysail
5 Foresail
6 Fore lower topsail
7 Fore upper topsail
8 Fore topgallant
9 Fore-royal
10 Main-topmast staysail
11 Main-topgallant staysail
12 Main-royal staysail
13 Mainsail
14 Main lower topsail
15 Main upper topsail
16 Main topgallant
17 Main royal
18 Trysail

Fredericks Sail Configuration

Barker was needed on deck, but he was suffering from chronic seasickness so he was no use to anyone. He wasn't the only one. Shires, Russen and the little runt Cheshire were all suffering terribly.

Under the worst possible conditions the *Frederick* was under control of five men: Lyon, Porter, Jones, Fare and Dady.

The normal tasks such as keeping watch, cooking meals and navigation were abandoned.

Hoy had built a magnificent ship. The *Frederick* had been tossed around like a child's toy, climbing and descending thirty-foot waves, yet she held together through it all.

After two days of bedlam, the sky became blue and the sea calmed, and although the sufferers of seasickness were still not well, life on deck became normal. The *Frederick* was now sailing under full sail, heading for Chile.

Despite the storm, the brig had made good progress over three hundred nautical miles. Barker was back on deck and driving the *Fredrick* as hard as it could go. He took a meridian observation of the sun's position on 16 January. He decided to alter the course to east by south.

To avoid shipping, they were heading for the Southern Ocean, which had a reputation for severely strong winds.

The crew were more than aware of what lay ahead: icy cold winds, huge seas and, with luck, no icebergs. They hoped Barker knew what he was doing. He spent most of his time in his cabin feeling ill. He didn't take daily readings so there was little faith they would make landfall in Chile.

The *Frederick* was meant to be heading for the port city of Valdivia. They chose Valdivia because it was a smaller port than Valparaiso, and therefore, they should be less conspicuous to the authorities.

They knew when they entered the Southern Ocean the seas would become rougher and the wind would blow harder. Barker was still suffering from seasickness as were a few of the crew.

Fare ordered the topgallants, the highest of the sails, to be reduced as he was concerned they were carrying too much sail in the conditions.

The crew were becoming nervous as they sailed south. They needed to sail north if they were to reach their destination safely.

'I don't like this. Barker stays in his fucking cabin day and night. He hasn't taken a reading for a week and we keep heading south,' said Jones.

'Aye, and did you see all that seaweed we passed through today? Seaweed means land yet we have weeks to go before we hit Chile,' said Leslie.

'I think we need to drag the bugger out of his sick bed so he can take a reading and reassure us all,' said Shires.

Two convicts, Shires and Leslie, knocked on Barker's door.

'What is it?' yelled Barker.

'It's Shires and Leslie. Can we come in? We'd like to talk to you.'

'Is it important? I feel ill.'

'It is very important.'

'All right. Come in.'

'Barker, we represent the crew. We are all concerned we are not heading for Chile and you haven't adjusted our direction for quite some time.'

'There's no need to worry, lads. I know what I'm doing.'

'We hope so. We saw a lot of seaweed yesterday and we're worried we'll make landfall south of Chile.'

'All right, I'll come up, but both of you need to help me.'

Once Barker was helped up to the main deck he took a reading and he also looked at the seaweed.

'Don't worry, men there's nothing to worry about. We are on course and making good speed.'

A week of good sailing passed. The mood on the ship was convivial but there was still concern Barker was not taking regular readings.

On January 31 Barker made an appearance, took a reading and announced that they needed to alter their course to northeast. The crew felt, at last, they were sailing for Chile.

GETTING CLOSER

CHAPTER 8

Having adjusted her course, the *Frederick* was now sailing in much calmer conditions in the southern Pacific. Nobody, including Barker, was sorry to leave the Southern Ocean behind.

The crewmember most excited was Fare. He could now raise full sails giving the brig real speed. The only downside was more speed meant more pumping, yet the crew didn't complain. They would be in Chile within four weeks.

Something else that lifted the spirits of the crew was the warm weather. Not so long ago many had icicles attached to their beards and frostbite on their fingers.

No one felt happier than Porter. He was free and sailing to Chile in a brig he helped build. The *Frederick* had performed beautifully. It was light and fast but handled the rough and the smooth equally.

Porter was standing on the main deck enjoying the light breeze when he looked out to the horizon and noticed some clouds moving quickly towards them. Porter was amazed at how quickly they were moving. Suddenly, the wind turned ferocious and the sea became a cauldron of black choppy water. The sails were shrieking like a banshee and then a huge wall of water hit the port side of the *Frederick* so hard she listed heavily to the starboard side.

The crew were being tossed around like rags dolls, desperately looking for something to hold on to.

Porter heard a loud crack and he looked up only to see the main boom crash into the sea, taking ropes and a sail with it.

The squall disappeared as quickly as it arrived, leaving the *Fredrick* and its crew in total disarray. Fare immediately ordered the majority of the sails down but he couldn't do anything about the broken spar. Repairs would have to wait for Chile.

Fare realised that they couldn't run the *Frederick* bare for too long. They needed momentum in case strong winds followed the squall so he ordered seventy percent of the sails to be unfurled.

Soon after, another storm hit, requiring the exhausted crew to climb the masts to lessen the sail again. A few crewmembers, including Lyon and Jones, decided life was possibly easier on Sarah Island.

When the storm abated and the sun came out they changed their minds as did the men who had remained below suffering chronic seasickness.

February 6

Barker was once again ill and in his cabin throughout the calamity but after a day of calm weather he came up on deck. He took a reading at 12 noon and made some navigation calculations.

'Mr Porter, would you please inform Mr Lyon to alter our course to north. We are too far south of the parallel. On our new course, we will reach Chile in a few weeks.'

Porter did as requested.

The *Frederick* was sailing smoothly and the crew was able to recover the broken spa as it was still attached to the ropes. It was repaired with a wooden splint.

Lyon was now enjoying his time at the wheel although his arms still ached from keeping the brig afloat during the squall and subsequent storm.

As he looked out to sea, he spied another ship sailing in their direction.

'Ship ahoy!' he yelled.

Porter grabbed the eyeglass to determine if it was a British warship, but it was still too far away to identify.

'Barker, what do you think? We may be able to outrun her.'

'I don't think we should panic just yet, Porter. It may be a Chilean vessel or maybe even a whaler.'

'I suppose you're right. We will probably encounter more ships as we get nearer to the coast.'

As the ships got nearer, they all gave a sigh of relief. It was a whaler and both ships just ignored one another.

February 25

'Land ho!' was the call from John Dady. The other crewmembers raced over to the port side, almost causing the ship to list. Sure enough, it was land, despite Barker's reckonings that put them 500 miles from Chile.

Barker took another sighting at noon and confirmed it was indeed Chile.

What an incredible feat! They had sailed six thousand nautical miles in a ship that hadn't cured and with a leak that necessitated constant pumping just to stay afloat. Not only that— it was manned by a crew of ten, half of which had no experience.

The crew of the *Frederick* were happy and sad; happy to reach Chile and a new life but sad that the *Frederick* would be beneath the ocean forever more. She was now leaking so badly that Porter estimated she would only be afloat for a few more hours.

He ordered the men to prepare the longboat for launching and ensure the sails were in good order.

They loaded the longboat with the remaining beef and biscuits. Finally, they added rifles, pistols and ammunition.

The *Frederick* was slowly sinking. Water was up to the ceiling of the galley and she made the noises of a ship that was dying.

Every man who sailed on the little brig was in despair when they watched the *Frederick* disappear under the ocean. She'd done them proudly through storm and tempest.

SAVED

CHAPTER 9

Hoy, Taw and the four soldiers knew they had to make a decision. They could stay where they were and hope a ship would be dispatched from Port Arthur looking to discover why the *Frederick* had not arrived at the new penal colony. The other option would be to head for Woolnorth Station where the Van Diemen's Land Company was headquartered. It was the only settlement in the north.

There was no guarantee a ship would arrive before their provisions ran out, therefore, they decided to make for Woolnorth Station a distance of approximately 170 miles through scrub, rivers and the strong possibility of aboriginal attack.

Hoy was ever grateful that Shires had given him a compass as without it they would all perish.

The group's first major hurdle was how to get to the northern end of the harbour. They had been left on the southern side.

Crossing Macquarie Harbour

'To swim across would be impossible and besides, I can't swim,' said Taw.

As it turned out only two of the party could swim so there had to be another way.

'Well, we'll have to build a boat, won't we?' said Hoy.

'How can we do that we don't have any tools?' said White, one of the soldiers.

'I think you all have forgotten I am a master shipbuilder. I think we should build a raft. There's plenty of wood around and the mutineers left us some twine.'

Hoy organised every member of the party to look for and bring back suitable branches and logs. Taw had a pocketknife, which was used to clean up the logs. It took a day to complete. Hoy decided that the craft could take three at a time. By the end of the day, all members of the group were on the northern side of the harbour with all their provisions.

They all had a fitful sleep that night but at least they had blankets, thanks to the mutineers.

The next morning after a delicious breakfast of tea and biscuits, they set off on what would be a long and arduous trek.

They chose to take the coastal route, which meant three days walking on sandy beaches, which had only been walked on by aboriginals for the past 50,000 years or more.

They reached a rocky outcrop and steep cliffs at the end of the third day, which precipitated them to head inland.

On the fourth day they crossed the Pieman River at low tide, which meant traversing across round river rocks without twisting an ankle.

The next few days were the most difficult, hacking their way through the dense rainforest. At the end of each day, sore and exhausted, they ate the meagre supplies that remained and endeavoured to find a dry patch to lie down.

Northern Tasmanian Rain Forest

January 24 1834

The party arrived at Woolnorth community, established by the Van Diemen's Company.

VDL has a long and entrenched place in Tasmanian history.... The 142,000-hectare tract of land included a 41,000-hectare parcel named Woolnorth, was the beginning of the Van Diemen's Land Company. The VDL property was also the scene of violent clashes with aboriginal people who were resisting the taking of their land.

The party staggered into the settlement, all exhausted, sunburnt and elated to have made it.

Two things ensured their survival; the generous amount of provisions supplied by the mutineers and the compass given to Taw by Shires.

Hoy caught a ship to Launceston, arriving in the thriving township three days after arriving at Woolnorth. He made a sworn statement to a magistrate detailing their experiences.

Captain Taw waited until he could arrange passage to Hobart. He arrived in the capital of the colony in the middle of February. Governor Arthur was very keen to hear his account of events.

There was keen interest by the townsfolk and the local newspaper reported:

COLONIAL TIMES.

Hobart Town:

PRINTED BY ANDREW BENT, ELIZABETH-STREET.

News has reached the town this morning, that the new schooner (sic) the Frederick, built at Macquarie Harbour, and which had been expected to arrive in Hobart Town for the past three weeks, has been piratically seized by the prisoners, left at the abandoned settlement, for the purpose of bringing the vessel to this port. Captain Taw arrived by ship this morning from Launceston, bringing the above intelligence. It appears the prisoners took advantage of some soldiers being on a fishing expedition when they overpowered the remainder and took forcible possession of the vessel.

The Frederick is spoken of as being a fast vessel, and as the pirates have had three weeks' start, there is little chance of their capture.

Governor Arthur was furious. He had penned strict Standing Orders for the Masters of Colonial Vessels. It seemed most of those orders had been ignored, hence the seizure of the Frederick. One of those orders and possibly the most critical were no convicts were allowed to handle any form of offensive weapon. Considering Barker was the penal settlement's gunsmith, he would have handled offensive weapons every day.

Other convicts used axes and other shipbuilding tools on a daily basis, and these too were classified as offensive weapons.

Somebody would have to pay for this fiasco.

185

The newspapers of the colony followed the government line. The ten convicts were pirates and would be hanged when caught.

The citizens of Hobart Town looked upon them differently; they praised the *Frederick* ten for their kindness and generosity in giving more than 50% of the available provisions.

Governor Arthur was not looking forward to reporting the seizure to his superiors in London; he knew they would not be impressed.

An official inquiry was ordered from London. Taw knew whose head would roll.

Ironically the Board of Inquiry sat in Hobart on March 5, the same day the crew of *Frederick* came ashore at Valdivia.

The Board found:

that no culpable blame attaches to the guard, it having placed itself under the direction of Captain Taw. The loss of the vessel can be accounted for only by the number of resolute convicts having associated together as to have enabled the organisation of the plan to take the Frederick and to the blind confidence placed in these people by Mr Hoy added to a like confidence on the part of Captain Taw whilst considering them as crew to which misfortune (this misplaced confidence) the court are of the opinion the success of the attack so easily carried is attributable.

Taw was dismissed from service Hoy would no longer be master shipwright at Port Arthur but was relegated to assisting in the construction of a lighthouse at South Bruny Island.

Terra Firma

Chapter 10

Once all ten convicts were in the longboat, they set forth, hugging the coast, and what a coast it was with rich thick rainforest down to the beach. After weeks at sea it was tempting to go ashore but Porter reminded the men their first priority was fresh water and food.

The seas had become rough and every man was soaking but they carried on. Porter knew they must head north if they were to find Valdivia.

As the longboat sailed along, passing bay upon bay, the men were becoming anxious. They still hadn't stepped onto to land yet; something they had all dreamed of for weeks.

At the end of the fourth day in the longboat, they found a perfect bay where they could land.

Porter guided the boat up on the beach and the men hopped out and began running along the shore. They were like schoolchildren experiencing a beach for the first time.

Porter and Barker were hoping they would find some civilisation, but it seemed the area was uninhabited.

There may not have been inhabitants but there were oysters and abalone and the crew were delighted to see something different from salted beef and rock hard biscuits. They ate well that night.

The next morning they set off again, hoping it would be the day they would arrive at Valdivia.

'Porter, you have lived in Chile before. How long before we get to whatever it's called?' asked Lyon.

'It's called Valdivia and how in the fuck would I know? I've never been in this part of Chile before.'

'Well, it seems every bay and inlet is the same— jungle and sand.'

'You've just got to be patient, Charles. We know we are heading in the right direction and it shouldn't be too much longer,' said Barker.

On the fifth day, they heard s familiar sound.

'Did you hear that?' asked Dady.

'It sounds like a cow,' said Russen.

'If it is there's bound to be people around,' said Porter.

Barker was at the tiller and he guided the boat close to shore. They could see people on the shore and the entire crew began yelling and waving at the Chileans.

The Chileans shouted back, but they sounded fierce and not welcoming at all. Porter and Barker decided to hold back until the next morning, despite not wanting to spend another night on the boat.

After a restless night, they brought the boat into shore. Porter and four others disembarked onto the beach while the other five stayed with the boat.

Porter led the expedition party up the beach when they saw several men hiding behind a large rock. These men were from the Mapuche people, an ancient indigenous race.

Porter adopted the international sign of peace. He held up his hands, as did the others. The men walked slowly towards Porter's party, stopping a dozen yards short. The Mapuche men all brandished long knives.

There was of cause a language barrier. The natives gesticulated and asked many questions none of which was understood or answered. Porter and his men rubbed their stomachs indicating, they hoped, that they required food.

The native men looked very fit and healthy as opposed to Porter's men who were unkempt with long dirty beards, clothing that was barely holding together and all as skinny as rakes.

Just when the Mapuche men were about to give up, a tall man dressed in bright clothing approached Porter. This man was the chief of the tribe.

Billy Shires walked up to the chief and respectfully handed him an axe. The chief was demonstrably pleased with the gift. He indicated to the white men to follow him. The other native men followed as they walked along the beach for a few hundred yards and then turned inland. After a short distance, they entered a clearing with a crystal clear stream running through it. Huts surrounded the clearing, all made of wood and straw. These people led a very well ordered life.

Porter still couldn't get the message through to the chief that he and his men were starving.

As they were leaving the village, Porter tried mentioning Valdivia on the basis that the Mapuche people may have heard of it.

A woman indicated she knew the town she held up three fingers and said

Leghos; three leagues, which equated to nine miles. The men were ecstatic as they now knew how far they needed to sail.

March 5 1834

The next afternoon they rounded another point but this point was different from all the others they had encountered over the previous days. Valdivia was before them, a beautiful harbour town.

The site of the town brought back memories to Porter. It was where he lived when he was eighteen. He had no intention of finding his wife and child as he knew his presence would not be welcome. After all, he abandoned them many years ago.

The harbour was deep blue and as calm as a millpond; surrounding the harbour were pine trees all the crew could smell the scent it was different to the eucalypts they were used to.

There were several small islands dotted around the harbour and mountains providing a backdrop to the town.

As they sailed towards the jetty, they passed an island that had a fort as its main feature. It appeared to have a twelve-gun battery.

The convicts tied up to the jetty, hoping they would be welcome visitors.

Many brightly dressed villagers and several soldiers resplendent in their blue uniforms welcomed them.

The pirates all looked at each other and grinned. They had achieved a near impossible journey from Van Diemen's Land to Valdivia, Chile, and they were free men. They could now enjoy life in a beautiful part of the world.

Porter and Barker had instructed the men to go by different names. John Barker became Benjamin Smith; William Cheshire was William Williams; Shires was now William Jones, and James Porter was James O'Connor.

The story was they were the survivors of the shipwreck *Mary* that went down after hitting rocks off the coast of Chile during a violent storm. Their home port was Liverpool, England.

The Chilean authorities accepted their story.

It became known that some of the men were carpenters. This was a skill in much demand, particularly in shipbuilding, and there was a large vessel sitting on the stocks waiting to be completed. The carpenters agreed to travel ten miles upriver and help finish the build. Cheshire went with them and

Porter was pleased to see him go as he didn't trust the bastard.

The remainder of the convicts stayed behind in Valdivia, intent on drinking, eating and lying with pretty Chilean women.

The carpentry group stayed in a village half way to their destination and they too drank and ate. It was during that time that one of the group divulged the true story of their escape on the *Frederick* to a man called Tom; an Englishman living in Valdivia. Nobody owned up to the indiscretion, but Cheshire was the chief suspect.

Porter and the rest of the men drank too much and ate too much and by 1 am they were all asleep in the sand on the main beach.

At 7 am Porter felt something hard against his chest. He looked up, only to find a soldier with his musket pointing at his heart. More soldiers had their muskets pointed at the other men also.

They were ordered to get to their feet. The five convicts were totally confused and bewildered, brushing sand from their clothes and wiping their eyes. Things couldn't get worse as all of them were suffering from chronic hangovers.

Porter, Jones, Fare, Leslie and Lyon were marched ten miles to the centre of Valdivia where they were imprisoned in a fortress called Cuartel. These men were unaware that the carpenters were also being held in a separate part of the fortress.

Porter had no idea why after being treated so kindly they had been locked up in a prison cell.

He understood enough Spanish to learn from a guard that one of their crew had divulged the true story, including their real names. His immediate suspicion was the little runt Cheshire but there was no proof of that.

After a week of detention, they were taken out to meet with the governor. They had not seen the town before and they were impressed with the Spanish architecture and the convergence of three rivers the Valdivia, the Calle-Calle and the Cruces.

The five convicts were ushered into the governor's office and again the *Frederick* men were most impressed. The walls of mahogany panels and the polished floors had an overall feel of opulence and officialdom.

Sitting at a large oak desk was a very distinguished looking man.

A government official signalled to the *Frederick* crew to sit at a very long board table. The governor rose from his desk, joining them at the head of the table.

Sitting next to the governor was an English sea captain known to be a notorious smuggler. His name was Captain Lawson. He was present at the meeting to act as an interpreter.

Porter was the spokesman for the group.

He related the story of the shipwreck of the *Mary* and how their brave captain went down with the ship, carrying with him the ship's papers.

'I find it very difficult to accept your explanation. My belief is you are pirates who murdered the captain and seized the ship. You then removed any traces of your actions and gutted the ship and took to the longboat.'

'I assure you, sir, that's not true. We are genuine shipwrecked sailors hoping for your hospitality while we remain in Chile,' pleaded Porter.

Cockney Tom was ushered into the office to give his opinion of the story being espoused.

'Sir, I believe the story being provided. I have no reason not to.'

The governor contemplated what had been said.

'Sailors, you have come on this coast in a clandestine manner and though you put a good face on your story, I have every reason to believe you are pirates. Unless you state the truth between this and tomorrow at eight o'clock, I shall give orders for you all to be shot. Take them away.'

Porter spoke using a nautical term. 'Avast there,' he said, addressing the governor. 'We are nothing but shipwrecked sailors in distress and expected when we arrived here to be treated like Christians, not like dogs.'

Porter displayed his patriot card to the governor.

'Would you have treated us this way in 1818 when we British sailors were helping you fight for your independence and bleeding for the cause?'

The governor remained silent.

Porter made it clear that he and his comrades had fought for Chile. Not only that, but they served under Admiral Thomas Cochrane nicknamed the Sea Wolf. The admiral was credited in Chile for helping it gain its independence from Spain.

Porter was pushing the truth. The others had never been to Chile before and half of them had never heard of it prior to the journey across the Pacific. He was determined not to be the only one spared from the firing squad.

'If you treat us as pirates, England will know of it and be revenged.

You will find us in the same mind tomorrow as we are now, and should you put your threat into execution, we shall teach you how patriots die!'

Porter was not known for his oratory skills, unlike William Swallow of the Cyprus. However, he excelled on this occasion.

The *Frederick* ten were returned to their cells to await the governor's decision. Overnight the true story of the *Frederick's* seizure and the voyage to Chile was leaked to the governor; by who wasn't divulged, but Porter suspected Cheshire. The little runt had negotiated a deal to save his neck.

The men decided now that the true story was known to go to the governor and tell their story as it happened.

'Was there bloodshed when the ship was seized?' asked the governor.

'None whatsoever, Your Excellency. We took care of our captives by taking them to the shore and providing them with more than 50% of our rations plus blankets, coats and most importantly a compass. We beg Your Excellency for clemency,' said Barker.

'I will release you on the condition you do not escape.'

'We agree, Your Excellency. I can assure you we'd rather be shot dead in the palace square than be delivered to the British Government,' Barker replied.

Cheshire was given protection in case the other men attacked him.

Good riddance, thought Porter. I don't want to see the little bastard again for as long as I live.

May 9 1834

The *Araucano* newspaper published a story about the convicts' exploits and a full description was reported. Somebody gave the article to a sea captain who was returning to Van Diemen's Land and it ended up in the hands of Governor Arthur.

It read in part:

It became clear that the shipwreck was false, that the individuals were criminals escaped from Van Diemen's Land in New Holland. By that which they have since disclosed it appears that they were occupied in the construction of vessels on account of Government in Port Macquarie [sic]; that the last being finished, which was a merchant ship called the Frederick, of little more than a hundred tons, all the prisoners embarked on her, with the captain, the mate, four soldiers and one free mariner.

The article went on to describe the seizing of the ship the voyage across the Pacific to South America and the sinking of the brig.

'What in the fuck do we do now? Everyone in Valdivia would have read this story by now, including the governor,' said John Jones.

'We've got no option but to plead for mercy on the basis we were harshly treated by the British authorities,' said Barker.

Barker and Porter requested an audience with the governor, which was granted. The two convicts arrived at the governor's office at 11am. They pleaded for mercy and assured His Excellency that if turned over to the British they would be tortured prior to being hanged.

The governor listened to their plea, showing empathy for their situation.

'I cannot make you any promises, but I will try to convince the Secretary of State for Foreign Affairs in Santiago that if you were returned to the British you would come to serious harm. I will recommend you all receive asylum.'

On 13 May a letter was dispatched to the Interior Minister.

The governor freed the *Frederick* 10 on parole. They were required to remain in Valdivia and report weekly to the police. They were all delighted; it was the next best thing to being free.

The convicts were looked upon as heroes as the people believed them to be beloved rebels fighting for a cause.

In Australia, they were looked upon as convict scum.

THE GOOD LIFE

CHAPTER 11

The men began working; Porter joined the crew on a government boat while others worked on the governor's private vessel. The shipyards were the place of work for a few of the others.

The carpenters Johns, Dady, Jones and Fare, were seconded to help build a sloop.

Sloop

The *Frederick* 10 had immersed themselves into the Valdivian lifestyle. They all enjoyed the food, the wine and the women. Within six months, five of the ten were married.

Barker was first one off the mark. He had met a very rich widow at a function held by the governor. His marriage was an elaborate affair attended by the governor and his wife. Barker was now for all intents and purposes a very wealthy man.

All the men who were betrothed were married with children back in England. Their attitude was it didn't matter, as they would never be returning home.

Governor Arthur was enraged. He had now received the newspaper article published in *Araucano* and was determined to capture the *Frederick* pirates and bring them to justice. He sent a dispatch to London asking for their assistance. London contacted the British Vice Consul in Valparaiso, Colonel John Walpole. He, of course, knew all about the *Frederick* 10. They had become Chilean heroes and a thorn in his side.

Walpole was a brash no-nonsense type of official similar to Governor Arthur; he promised himself that he would see all these men hang for their heinous crime.

Walpole received a letter from the Chilean Secretary of State for Foreign Affairs, Don Joaquin Torconal, explaining what had happened and why the ten men were free on parole.

This sent Walpole into a rage. He wrote to the British Foreign Secretary, Viscount Palmerston in London. He described how the ten escaped convicts had made a full confession and therefore should be brought to justice instead of enjoying the good life in Valdivia.

The Chileans were more than aware that if the men were handed over to the British they would be executed. It was with this in mind that Tocornal wrote to Walpole explaining that a petition asking for the *Fredrick* 10's asylum had been received and he was obligated to give it due consideration.

His reason centred on the shocking conditions the convicts had to endure in Van Diemen's Land. He also intimated that the Chilean Government and its people did not endorse slavery, which was what the convict system was.

Tocornal requested a report stating what crimes each of the men had committed in England; he suspected they were fairly minor.

'As the Government of Chile has yet to be apprised of the nature of their crimes and the reason why they were condemned to the place where they were expelled, it cannot make a determination about the future fate of these wretched individuals; there are no other means by which we can arrive at the facts of the case other than via your proofs.'

Walpole responded with a request to lock up these despicable creatures in chains until the British Government could furnish proof of their atrocious crimes.

A presumption of guilt went against Chilean law. Walpole's request was denied.

Tocornal knew if he arrested the men there would be protests from the population of Valdivia, for they were very popular.

'I have the very strong feeling that the Government of Chile and the British Government are negotiating our arrest,' said Barker.

'I think you're right, John, and even though I'd like to think we'll be able to stay here permanently I think things could go south,' said Porter.

'A fellow came to me today, a Captain West. His ship has been impounded for carrying contraband. He wanted me to repair some rifles.'

'What's the name of the ship?'

'Ocean.'

'Why did he want you to repair the rifles?'

'He thinks several of his crew turned him into the port authorities and he wants his revenge,' said Barker.

' When's he due back to see you?'

'Tomorrow.'

'Why don't we propose to him that we provide nine experienced crew to sail his ship past the battery and out to sea?'

'Nine? We have ten.'

'We're not going to include that little snitching runt Cheshire are we?'

'No, you're right. He can stay behind and fend for himself.'

The following morning, Captain West came to John Barker's gun workshop. Barker convinced him that their plan would work and the Englishman agreed.

The following night being a quarter moon was chosen for the daring escape.

The plan was to steal one of the boats from the beach and row it out of the harbour to rendezvous with the *Ocean*.

The three men building the sloop had a much easier task. They would hide down below until nightfall and sail the yacht to meet the *Ocean*.

The six men in the rowboat had to make their way down the Rio Valdivia ten miles to the port, then out to the ship. They made good headway despite the current being against them and they reached the mouth of the river just as dawn was breaking. Unfortunately for them, the bar was a turbulent swirling mass with waves over six foot high.

They tried several times to get through the treacherous surf but were repelled each time. They finally realised it was futile. The three men in the sloop had been successful and were now sailing away in the *Ocean*.

The six men returned to Valdivia and were at their jobs by the normal start time. No one was the wiser of their attempted escape.

The three that boarded the *Ocean* made their way to Callao, Peru. John Dady stayed, while John Fare and John Jones boarded an American vessel, never to be heard of again.

Barker and Porter were fearful that the seven remaining convicts would be incarcerated or at least have their movements restricted because of the escape. They didn't need to worry. The governor seemed oblivious to the escape, and therefore, life went on as usual.

Walpole was not about to give up on apprehending the hideous thieving pirates. He was appalled by the fact that these felons were being treated like heroes right under his nose.

It flew in the face of British justice and he was determined to do something about it despite Santiago's complicity in their freedom.

He saw his opportunity when a British warship, the *Blonde,* visited Valparaiso. She was a forty-six-gun frigate, and a formidable weapon of the British Navy. Walpole invited the captain, Commodore Mason, to his villa for lunch, and he asked the Commodore to sail the four hundred-and-fifty nautical miles to Valdivia and encourage the governor to hand over the scoundrels. What Walpole was proposing was some British gunboat diplomacy.

'The sight of your guns pointing at the governor's residence should persuade him to release these pirates into your custody,' said Walpole.

'I would imagine he will be most cooperative, Vice Consul. If not, we'll fire a few cannon balls in his general direction,' said Commodore Mason.

The *Blonde*

The *Blonde* sailed into the harbour of Valdivia, anchoring with the starboard guns facing the governor's residence. Commodore Mason ordered a longboat with twelve men aboard to be lowered and rowed to the beach in front of the town.

As the boat approached the harbour fort, a 32-pound canon ball crossed her bows. It was obvious they were not welcome. The longboat returned to the *Blonde* as fast as the sailors could row.

When the governor heard of the incident he summoned the seven men and confined them in cells, not to imprison them, but rather to protect them.

'Good evening, gentlemen I apologise for the accommodation, but it's for your own protection.'

'Don't apologise, Governor de la Cavareda. We all appreciate your support, sir,' said Porter.

I have received a request from the ship's master for you all to go on board his ship and give an account of yourselves. Do you wish to go?'

'We will never render ourselves to the British under any circumstances.'

'Therefore, I will send Commodore Mason a letter inviting him to Government House where I will invite him to interview you all. There will be one proviso. He must come alone.'

Thank you, sir, but what if they come in numbers to take us away?'

'I will send you into the jungle where they will not find you.'

The letter was received by Commodore Mason and he was not impressed.

He did not answer the letter. Instead, he sailed back to Valparaiso, much to Walpole's disappointment.

The men knew it would not be the last British warship to visit Chile. Their time in this beautiful country was limited.

THE ORIGIN OF THE SPECIES

CHAPTER 12

Porter was enjoying not only his newfound freedom but also the status he held in the community. He was referred to as Don Santiago and he was known for his kindness and friendliness and willingness to help others. This was diametrically opposed to the piratical scum the British considered him.

Porter worked at the shipyards initially as a caulker and then as a rigger. He was then hired by his landlord, Don Lopez, who ran a furrier business. Don Lopez thought the world of Porter, taking him under his wing.

He asked Porter to collect a large quantity of skins from poachers upriver. Porter was chosen because of his sailing expertise. He and Don Santiago travelled up the Rio Primero to the point where they were due to collect and load the skins.

The river had significant rapids and Porter navigated the boat through with great skill and dexterity. All the skins made it back to port, though the norm was for some to be lost in the rapids and whirlpools.

There was an instance where Porter went to court to give testimony against a sealer and three soldiers who conspired to murder him.

He asked the court to show them mercy, and they were let off with a light sentence. His reputation grew and grew as a man of compassion.

Porter, Barker and the other five convicts knew that while they were enjoying the good life, Walpole was working hard to capture them and send them back to England so they could be hanged. They also knew Tocornal was working hard to protect them.

Walpole and Tocornal had become adversaries and a diplomatic incident between Britain and Chile was looming.

Walpole was furious with the Chileans firing upon one of Britain's finest warships. He saw it as almost an act of war.

Tocornal had an opposing view. Britain had sent a warship to a Chilean port and threatened to fire upon the town. He saw the Chilean response as natural.

Walpole demanded to know if all ten pirates were still in Chilean custody.

Tocornal informed him that three had escaped.

Walpole responded with venom. He wanted to know how and when they escaped and who was the recalcitrant who let them escape. He insisted the person responsible be charged immediately.

He then insisted that the remaining seven be incarcerated in chains until their guilt or innocence was determined.

Walpole was horrified to learn that some of the men had married Chilean women and were living a happy life, free as a bird.

One concession Tocornal made was to conduct an investigation into how the three men escaped.

As for the remaining seven in Valdivia, their lives would remain the same.

The *Frederick* seven were becoming increasingly nervous that the Chilean Government would capitulate to British pressure and they began hatching another escape plan.

In January, they received the news that their much-admired Governor Cavareda had been recalled to Santiago, to be replaced by Don Isaac Thompson.

When Governor Cavareda introduced Thompson to the men he assured them nothing would change and that he too would endeavour to win them asylum.

Porter was sceptical. There was something about the new governor he didn't like.

When Porter first met him he asked about his English surname. The new Governor explained he was Chilean of British descent. That set off some alarm bells.

Porter's misgivings about Thompson proved to be founded when he increased the reporting regime to daily at six o'clock. He also made a lame excuse as to why the men's asylum papers had been delayed.

Porter, Barker and the other five men were disturbed when they saw an English barque sail into the harbour. It wasn't a warship, but nevertheless, it was a British ship which was more than capable of taking the men back to England for trial and hanging. The name on its stern was HMS *Beagle* and it was on a voyage of discovery with a botanist called Charles Darwin.

H.M.S. "BEAGLE." [Frontispiece

The captain of the *Beagle* was Robert Fitzroy. He made no inquiries about the *Frederick* pirates, nor did Thompson offer any information as to their status or the circumstance that brought them to Valdivia.

Charles Darwin

Charles Darwin, on the other hand, knew all about the seizure of the *Frederick* the sinking of the brig and the fact that a number of the scoundrels had married local women. He saw them as rogues; nothing more, and besides, he was more interested in the local flora and fauna.

John Barker was a very astute man. He could read a situation better than most. He was also a meticulous planner and it was he who conceived the seizure of the *Frederick*. He was feeling uneasy about staying in Valdivia despite his happy marriage and the birth of a child. He felt that if they didn't move soon they would end up hanging in chains on the Thames.

James Porter, although nowhere as meticulous as Barker, had the same feeling. His instinct told him it was time to go.

Barker came up with a plan. He approached Governor Thompson, suggesting the men build him a whaleboat for sailing close to the coastline for his pleasure. Thompson was aware of how skilled the Englishmen were and agreed to the proposal.

Barker and his crew started immediately, and four weeks later they had built a fine vessel.

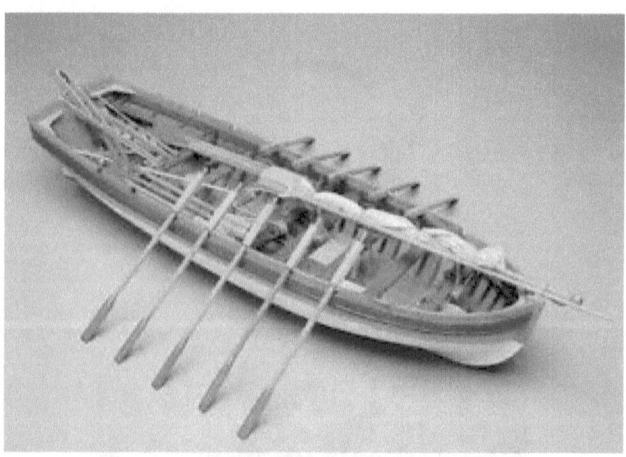

Porter and Barker met at Barker's villa.

'Porter, the plan is to take the boat downriver to the harbour on Sunday night and sail away under a dark moon. The authorities won't know we have gone until Monday,' said Barker.

'It sounds good, John. Has everyone agreed to go?'

'No, it's just going to be you, me, Russen and Leslie.'

'So the others want to stay?'

'Something like that.'

Porter was aware Shires' wife had just given birth, and therefore, he was probably reluctant to leave her.

As for the other two, Cheshire and Lyon, he suspected Barker just didn't want them in the boat.

Porter had a restless night thinking about the incredible journey he had been on over the previous two years and nervous about what the future held.

He headed for the port early Sunday evening to rendezvous with his fellow escapees but when he reached the spot where the governor's whaleboat had been moored, it wasn't there. He walked the harbour shore, hoping the boat had been moved and Barker had forgotten to inform him but alas, the whaleboat was nowhere to be seen.

He walked up the steep road to Barker's villa, which overlooked the entire town and the harbour. He knocked on the door and after several minutes Barker's wife answered the door.

'Hola Senora, I was wondering if I could talk to John?'

'I'm sorry, James he left last night. He was concerned the governor was intending to hand him and the men over to the British authorities.'

'It was meant to be tonight.'

'I'm sorry, James.'

Porter felt totally dejected. Why had he been left behind? What had he done to deserve this treatment?

Barker, Russen and Leslie rowed the boat quietly down the river until they reached the bar. All was calm, unlike the first attempt and they rowed out into the ocean. Barker was the captain and navigator, and he headed north hoping to make landfall in America. It is assumed they made it, as they were never heard of again.

The stealing of the whaleboat put a different perspective on things. Government property had been stolen.

Porter awoke the following morning to the sound of loud banging on his front door. He quickly got out of bed, hoping it was Barker coming back to take him away. To his astonishment, it was several soldiers who were going to take him away—but not to a life of freedom. He was taken to the fort's prison and chained to his good mate Billy Shires. The two others in the cell were Lyon and Cheshire the little scumbag.

When Walpole heard that an additional three pirates had escaped he was furious. He couldn't believe the Chileans could be that incompetent. Tocornal was very apologetic. This time, however, he insisted that he could not hand over the remaining men, as it would mean all four would be hanged. He did not interpret the convicts' actions as piracy but a bid for freedom.

Porter and Shires had been chained together for the past seven months. They were both filthy having not washed for the whole time in gaol. Both of them were depressed with their situation; they knew it would only be a matter of time before they were handed over to the British.

Don Lopez, Porter's good friend, paid him a visit, but the news he brought was not good.

'James, my friend, I'm afraid to tell you a British ship is on its way to pick you up and take you back for trial.'

Porter decided he must escape, but how?

He devised a plan. The first stage was to feign sickness and request to be unshackled from Shires. The prison warden agreed, but instructed the guards to fit irons to his ankles which prevented him from shuffling more than four inches at a time. He remained this way for seven weeks then, in a stroke of luck, a young girl Porter had saved from torture by her cruel female boss made a visit. Her name was Antoinetta and when she saw Porter she burst into tears.

'How could they do this to you of all people? You are such a kind and compassionate man.'

'Antoinetta, you can help me get out of here. Are you willing to assist me?'

'Of course, how can I help?

'Can you bring me a knife and a file?'

'Yes I will. When do you need them?'

'The next visiting day is on Friday.'

Antoinetta hid the file in her long red hair and the knife in the sleeve of her gown.

Porter was able to cut through his ankle chains within an hour. He asked permission to use the toilet and it didn't take long to scale the prison wall with the aid of a plank.

The prison guards observed the prisoner scale the walls and were soon in pursuit. He was able to evade them, and he then headed for the Rio Valdivia, which he needed to cross. He found a small dinghy and a paddle but just as he was set to launch a burly man shouted for him to stop. The paddle came in handy and the man was left on the riverbank unconscious.

He proceeded across the river. The evening was becoming very cold and his wet prison uniform didn't offer any warmth whatsoever.

He decided to move inland towards woods. He knew it would be less populated although the chances were he would come across the Mapuche. He hoped they would be friendly.

Porter fell asleep under a large Chilean pine tree which offered protection from the rain.

Next morning, cold and hungry, he came across a small farmhouse. He knew he had to take the risk; either that or die.

He knocked on the front door. An old lady opened it. She looked at Porter's sorry state and let him in. She served up several dishes, all of which he devoured.

Once he had eaten enough, she cleared the plates.

'Now, may I ask who you are and what are you running from?'

Porter made up some story involving a Frenchman.

'I don't believe it. You are Santiago. Don't worry. I will help you. I have no love for the governor or his soldiers.'

The woman provided a fresh set of clothes for Porter and a few days' food rations.

Porter walked and walked and by the fourth day he was exhausted. He needed to climb a small mountain, but unfortunately, he did a complete circle and after six hours of climbing, he found himself at the point where he began the climb.

Under the shadow of Villarrica volcano, he lay down and went to sleep.

Porter kept walking next day, hoping he would soon reach Concepcion, his final destination.

Two days later, soldiers found him exhausted by the road, just fifty miles from Concepcion.

His escape was reminiscent of his daring escapes in Van Diemen's Land and unfortunately it had the same result.

Once back in Valdivia, he was brought before Governor Thompson.

'Why did you run away?' asked Thompson.

'Two reasons I had for doing that. First the cruel treatment and oppression of a tyrant like yourself, and secondly with the hope of obtaining my liberty.'

'I see. Well, you are to be taken from here to have iron bars welded around your legs. Tomorrow you will be taken to the square and shot. Good day to you. I won't see you again.'

The townspeople, once they heard of Porter's sentence, marched on the governor's residence, pleading for him to spare Porter's life.

He reluctantly agreed and instructed a padre to inform the luckless Porter of his reprieve.

'Thank you, padre, but if it's all the same to you, I'm quite happy to meet my maker. I'm sick of this life.' Porter was obviously depressed.

Thompson visited Porter in his cell, expecting gratitude and thanks from the once condemned prisoner. What he got was, 'I will not thank you for prolonging a life like mine, which has been a life of misery. No, I will not thank you because you are the chief cause of it by your oppression.'

April 1836

As the town was enjoying its afternoon siesta, Porter, Shires, Lyon and Cheshire were escorted to the dock in chains. They were transferred to a British cutter, the HMS *Basilisk*.

Once on board, they were under British custody a fate they had endeavoured to avoid for two long years.

Back to Old Blighty

CHAPTER 13

The convoluted journey began; the prisoners were treated the same way as cargo transferred from ship to ship.

The first transfer was from the *Basilisk* to the HMS *Blonde*, which was anchored at Valparaiso. The *Blonde* then sailed to Callao in Peru.

'It seems a little ironic, mates, that we're on the same fucking ship that came to take us away eighteen months ago,' said Porter.

'To be honest I don't care what fucking ship we're on. The result will be the same.'

'You're right, Shires. The hangman's noose beckons.'

Porter's obsession to escape hadn't left him and he devised a plan to jump ship when the *Blonde* anchored in the next port.

He knew how to 'oval' his shackles and slip his feet out. Initially all four had decided to escape but when the time came only Porter attempted the breakaway.

Porter did reach the main deck but was apprehended soon after, so it was not his best attempt.

Captain Mason had him brought to his cabin for questioning.

' Porter, who was involved in your ill-conceived escape?'

'Just me.'

'Why did you try to escape?'

'I've been a prisoner most of my adult life. I've had enough. I am an innocent man, and therefore, I reserve my right to escape.'

'It is natural for a man to make his escape. It is our duty to prevent him.'

Mason didn't order Porter to be flogged. He was taken back down to the gun deck and chained to his good friend Shires and his mortal enemies Cheshire and Lyon who he suspected were guilty of alerting the guards.

The four were transferred to the *North Star* for their longest and final leg, rounding Cape Horn in freezing conditions. The captain negotiated the ship between icebergs and blue whales. The *North Star* sailed up along the South American coast to Rio de Janeiro, which would be the last port of call before

Portsmouth.

Porter hadn't seen old England for over ten years and he didn't miss her at all. The four convicts were assigned to a guard ship; a horrible existence where they were handcuffed to a grate and couldn't fend for themselves at all. Privacy while going to the toilet was a thing of the past. After two days, they were transferred to the enormous hulk of the *Leviathan*.

This once magnificent warship had seventy-two guns and was only second in importance to the *Victory* in Lord Nelson's fleet. Now it had become a dirty stinking hulk capable of holding over six hundred prisoners.

Leviathan War Ship

Leviathan Prison Hulk

The four prisoners knew the routine, as all had been imprisoned on hulks before they were transported to Australia. First was a bath, which was not unwelcome, then a new uniform comprising trousers, waistcoat and jacket was provided. Porter had the audacity to ask what colours were available and he got a smack on the head with a baton for his cheekiness.

December 21 1836

The remaining four *Frederick* pirates were transferred to the *Sarah*, a 480-ton transport ship. Her destination was Hobart Town in Van Diemen's Land. The four men were taken down into the hold where a vast array of criminals and political prisoners waited to greet them. Their ruthless reputations preceded them by accounts that they were all murdering scoundrels, pirates of the worst kind. Where these rumours came from Porter and his comrades had no idea, but it did serve a purpose as no other prisoner dared to offend them.

The *Sarah* took the normal route and they made port in Cape Town to take on fresh water and supplies and then rounded the Cape of Good Hope to catch the Roaring Forties, and then onto the next port of call at Hobart Town.

There were two significant events during the voyage. The first was an outbreak of erysipelas, known as red skin disease. This disease is normally not fatal but in the cramped putrid conditions of the *Sarah's* hold it spread like wildfire and nine prisoners died.

The captain feared a mutiny led by the four *Frederick* pirates and he decided to act before these scoundrels tried to take the ship.

The first prisoner to be hauled up on deck was Porter. He was followed by a large group of prisoners and it had become a mass gathering. Captain Whiteside, his officers and the ship's surgeon were all standing on the quarterdeck, looking down on the rabble.

It was Porter's good friend Shires who was pulled out first, and the look on the poor man's face was one of bemusement.

Captain Whiteside addressed the poor man.

'I believe you are the ringleader of this attempted mutiny. I sentence you to forty-eight lashes.'

'Tie him to the grate,' ordered the First Lieutenant.

A huge black sailor would administer the punishment.

Shire was brave. He didn't scream, but by the twelfth stroke he was moaning loudly.

By the time he had received the forty-eight strokes, he was a bloody mess and unconscious. Porter, looking on, feared for his good mate's life.

Porter was next. He, unlike Lyons, had experience with the cat. He'd received three hundred in his prison lifetime.

Porter pleaded his innocence but to no avail; Lyon and Cheshire stepped forward.

'These men are at the head of a vast and dangerous mutiny. Their plan was to rush the quarterdeck and slaughter everyone in sight,' shouted Lyon.

Porter's suspicions had been proved to be correct. These two would pay for their treachery one day, he thought as he was being tied to the grate.

The huge sailor used all his strength on the first stroke, breaking skin. By the time Porter had received forty-eight he hadn't taken his eyes off Captain Whiteside; nor did he utter a sound. He was taken down a bloody mess.

In all, sixty prisoners were named by their accusers as being complicit in the planned mutiny.

Three hours of floggings ensued and the decks ran red.

Things didn't get any better for Porter and Shires. They were thrown into a small dungeon, chained together at the ankle and with their hands tied behind their backs. To add insult to injury, Lyon and Cheshire had been appointed their guards.

After three weeks in purgatory the two men were brought up on deck, the sunlight blinding their eyes. The sailors on the deck looked at them in sympathy for the two men looked like the walking dead. They did not return to the hole but re-joined the general prison population.

Finally, the *Sarah* sailed into Storm Bay. In a few hours, they would be offloaded at the Port of Hobart Town. Porter knew they would be measuring him up for a coffin as soon as he arrived.

One good thing had happened since his departure; Governor Arthur had been replaced by Sir John Franklin, a much more compassionate man.

Sir John Franklin

Hobart Town Courier March 31 1837

THE HOBART TOWN COURIER.

This Journal contains every Official Notice in the Hobart Town Gazette.

the same place.

Several articles and communications, part of the Gazette, and reports of the Court, are unavoidably postponed.

The Courier.

FRIDAY MORNING, APRIL 17, 1835.

We have this week the melancholy task to detail one of the most awful and unforeseen visitations of Providence that frail and mortal man is subject to. The convict ship *George the Third*, of 400 tons, Captain W. Moxey, sailed for this place from London on the 14th of December, with 220 convicts, and a guard commanded by Major Ryan, of the 50th Regiment, with Lieut. Minion, Assistant Surgeon M'Gregor, and 29 rank and file. The vessel made the land on Sunday last, about 11 in the morning, and in coming up D'Entrecasteaux's channel, the weather being fine, and the vessel going at an easy rate in the moonshine, after passing all the reefs, called the

evidence taken on the inquiry, and it clearly appeared that he was entirely justified as a seaman in the course he had chosen, the charts and sailing directions in Horsburgh fully authorising it. In passing the reef all the usual precautions of sounding, &c. were regularly taken, and when the depth was under 20 fathoms, the deep sea lead was substituted by the hand lead. His deposition went on to the following effect:—

' When we got under 20 fathoms, I kept the soundings going with a hand lead. In passing between the 2 reefs laid down in the charts, I carried 7½ fathoms through. When we were past these reefs, I took my officers and passengers into the cabin and shewed them the position of the ship. We all felt satisfied that we had passed every danger, and concluded that we might proceed with safety under easy sail, the moon being clear and the weather mild—going from a knot and a half to 2 knots an hour. She was at that time under double reefed topsails, with the foresail hauled up, all ready for coming to an anchor, should it become dark. After proceeding on for about a quarter of an hour, I was walking on the weather side of the poop, when the man in the chains heaving the lead, called out quarter less four. I immediately desired him to put the helm hard to port—the distance from the

did not see any shoal near on the starboard. Their conduct during the voyage was very good. As soon as the ship struck the prison between decks broke down, and the prisoners came out as fast as they could, all hands trying to save themselves; many were washed off. There was no heavy swell before the vessel struck. There were flying clouds and was struck, with the wind off the land; it was not a hazy night—the moon shone bright. I believe two of my men had been up the chain net before, but I could not obtain any information from them. I depended solely on my charts and Horsburgh's directions. I considered that my third mate in the gig had been swamped, as I did not see him any more. I met with all possible assistance and support from every one on board, that had it in his power to help. Some of the prisoners were themselves particularly useful, and went with me to and from the shore—Nelson, Jones, and Shaw, and many others whose names I can recollect, persevered to the utmost to assist me.

Dr. Wyse, the Surgeon-Superintendent was next examined. He deposed as follows:— The sinking of the land was received with much joy by all on board. The captain and officers and myself had agreed during the voyage to proceed through D'Entrecasteaux's channel. On a former voyage in 1833 I had

Porter, Lyon and Cheshire, who have been sent here to take their trial for seizing a vessel, the Frederick. During the voyage, a plan was formed, in which a freeman, a sailor on board, is involved to take the Sarah; but as is invariably the case, the plot was disclosed to the officers and accordingly frustrated.

The *Frederick* prisoners were taken to the police barracks and checked for identifying scars, tattoos etc. Once that task was completed they were marched up to Hobart Gaol in Murray Street. They were allocated a cell each and that's where they would reside for the next month.

Hobart Gaol

TRIALS AND TRIBULATIONS

CHAPTER 14

The day of the trial had arrived and all four defendants were extremely nervous. The Solicitor General, Edward Macdowell, would represent the Crown. Nobody would represent the *Frederick* four.

The visitors' gallery was full; as in William Swallow's trial in London, there was a crowd waiting outside the court.

Everybody wanted to see the swashbuckling pirates that sailed to Chile.

At 9 am Justice Pedder entered the court, taking his seat on the bench.

There was a sense of excitement in the courtroom. The people saw a case like this as entertainment. There wasn't much else to do in Hobart Town.

The dinner conversations in Hobart Town since the four arrived centred around, 'Are they saints or sinners?'

The jury were twelve men dressed in military uniform; not a good sign for the accused.

Justice Pedder instructed for the four accused to enter the courtroom and as they approached the dock there were murmurings in the public gallery. The gallery's expectations were deflated when instead of their vision of romantic pirates what they saw was four scrawny convicts, all looking very sheepish.

Three indictments were read out. The most serious was the charge of piracy. If found guilty, they would all hang.

The charges were:

'Piratically and feloniously carrying away on the 13th January 1834 the brig *Frederick*, Charles Taw master, belonging to our Sovereign Lord the King and of the estimated value of £1200, from the high seas, to wit, Macquarie Harbour on the coast of Van Diemen's Land.'

The second count was that of breaking their trust as sworn mariners. The third was the same as the first except in did not state Charles Taw to be a subject of William IV.

Justice Pedder turned to the four prisoners. 'How do you plead?'

All four pleaded not guilty.

David Hoy was called to the stand. When asked his profession he replied, 'shipbuilder.'

When asked if he knew all the defendants he replied, 'I do.'

The solicitor general, Edward Macdowell, asked Hoy to tell the court what happened on 13 January 1834.

He recounted all the events of the day including the seizure.

He was asked who pointed the pistol at him.

'It was William Shires.'

Hoy went recounting the altercation in Taw's cabin and the aftermath.

When asked who was the ringleader giving the orders he replied he didn't know.

He made it clear to the court by his evasive answers that he was not going to give any of them up.

Finally, Macdowell asked Hoy who was the mastermind behind the plot.

'I believe it was Barker.'

Unfortunately for Macdowell, he would never have Barker in court.

In the end, he told the court that he and Captain Taw had given themselves up to the convicts for fear of their lives.

Justice Pedder adjourned for lunch. After the break, he had some questions.

These questions related to who was in charge, the nature of the men's employment, when the *Frederick* was launched and the geography of Macquarie Harbour.

'Did you consider the vessel was on the high seas when she was taken?' Pedder asked Hoy.

'I do not.'

'Were the convicts employed as seamen?'

'They were not hired nor were they paid for their work. They did perform the duties of a seaman.'

Macdowell called on Billy Shires to testify, and Hoy remained in the witness stand.

'May it please the court to know that we had all offered the captured men food and provisions and had never seriously threatened any of them,' stated Shires.

Pedder showed no reaction to Shire's statement.

'Could you confirm, Mr Hoy, that when you were in your cabin getting your clothes, I had given you a pocket compass and said I was sorry I could not give you more?'

Shires also asked Hoy to confirm that he had wrapped up a bottle of spirits in his shirt and told him to put it out of sight.

'Could you confirm that you were put on shore with eighteen pounds of meat, twenty-six pounds of biscuits, and six pounds of flour?' Shires asked.

Hoy confirmed Shires' claim and added a live goat, cooking pans and an axe.

Shires was appealing to the court for its sympathy as he went on to say, 'We all felt compelled to take the *Frederick* as Captain Taw threatened to put us ashore while he was in a drunken stupor. It was a condition he was permanently in.'

These claims were not confirmed by Hoy.

Next to testify was Lyon. He didn't have much to say of significance and was excused.

Next up was Porter. He reiterated what Shires had said about the generosity of the convicts to their captives. He also explained that the provisions on board were adequate for the journey from Macquarie Harbour to Port Arthur, but certainly not for a journey to Chile yet they gave more than half the ship's provisions away.

His last statement was directed to Hoy.

'Did you not say that the humanity and kindness you had received from the prisoners was so great and unexpected, that you could not forget it?'

Hoy confirmed he had indeed said this.

Porter returned to the dock and next up was William Cheshire.

The little runt, as Porter called him, simply asked whether Hoy thought him of good character.

Hoy agreed.

The final witness was James Tate, Captain Taw's first mate.

He had not had any exposure to the four accused prior to the seizure. The day of the seizure he was treated badly so he wasn't going to be gentle with his testimony.

'Who was the most provocative of these men?' asked Macdowell.

'Russen was running around with a tomahawk and Shires had presented a pistol to me and said, 'not a word or I'll blow your brains out.'

'What about Porter?'

'I didn't see him with any arms but it was he who tied me up with great force.'

Cross-examined by Lyon, Tate agreed Taw was drunk on the day the ship was launched and often was inebriated.

'Was Captain Taw drunk the day the ship was seized?' asked Lyon.

'He was in a state of perfect sobriety,' Tate responded.

The four convicts' defence just got weaker.

Summing Up

It was time for the accused to sum up their cases.

The first to stand and address the court was Lyon.

'I was forced to stay with the convicts because I was the only one who had any real knowledge of the coast.' He had decided to emulate William Swallow's line of defence.

Shires was next; he explained that he entered the captain's cabin with a pistol in hand to save Taw and Hoy from possible harm. This was an argument few in the court believed.

Shires also asserted that the *Frederick*, 'did not come within the description of a vessel; it was a mere raft and was not registered.'

Porter knew their situation was hopeless. He and his men would throw themselves upon the mercy of the court.

'Nobody has any idea of the hardships we had to endure before we finally made it to South America. It was indescribable what was happening at Macquarie Harbour. And when we reached Chile we gave ourselves up to the government there.

The gallery and indeed the court could empathise with what Porter was saying. What normal man would not try to escape the horrors of Sarah Island?

The Hobart Town Courier in an article wrote that Lyon and Porter were intelligent men while Shires was quiet and unassuming. Cheshire was described as a 'weak lad'.

The four convicts were pessimistic as with a military jury the chances of a not guilty verdict was remote.

Justice Pedder now asked the jury to consider some points, which hadn't been raised in the trial before they took their leave to consider their verdict.

'You need to decide whether the *Frederick* was seized on the high seas or not. Are you sure Macquarie Harbour constitutes a harbour or an estuary or was it indeed the high seas? If you decide it was the high seas then these men are pirates.

'The other important point to be considered is the brig *Frederick* had never been registered.

'You, the men of the jury, need to consider if these four prisoners were actually mutineers when the unregistered ship technically wasn't at sea and Captain Taw had yet to take command.'

A SHIP OR NOT A SHIP

THAT IS THE QUESTION

CHAPTER 15

Pedder endeavoured to make it perfectly clear to the jury that their verdict must rely on a proper point of law.

The law stated that once a ship's anchor was lowered into a harbour all legal powers she had enjoyed at sea ceased. Therefore the *Frederick* four could not be considered pirates.

In relation to the *Frederick* it was always described as a brig of 130 tons but was it really a ship?

In legal terms the 'vessel', said to have been 'piratically carried away', possessed nothing that would bring her within the legal definition of the term 'ship'. She had not been commissioned or registered and no warrant had been issued for the vessel.

Pedder described it as; 'it was legally little more than a quantity of wood and other materials so fastened as to possess the means of becoming a brig, but possessing no one constituent necessary to justify those materials being then so-called'.

To add to the argument, Barker disposed of the ship's papers relating to the vessel off the coast of South America when the *Frederick* was sunk. In the eyes of the law, the ship never existed.

The old saying goes that if it looks like a duck, swims like a duck and quacks like a duck it's probably a duck.

In this case, the *Frederick* may have looked like a ship, felt like a ship and sailed like one, but it wasn't one at all.

The flaws in the prosecution's case for piracy against the four both geographically and in law looked weak.

The other part of the charge was mutiny.

To be a mutineer one needed to be a mariner and the *Frederick* four were prisoners.

There needed to be someone in charge of the ship when the mutiny took place. Taw wasn't technically in command of the *Frederick* when it had been seized. Nor were they on the high seas. They were in Macquarie Harbour.

The fact of the matter was there was no person in command to commit the mutiny against. Nor were there any sailors aboard to commit the mutiny; therefore, no mutiny took place.

The four prisoners realised that it had been serendipity that they seized the *Frederick* when they did. They should be charged with robbery and no more.

The twelve military men retired to consider their verdict and the four prisoners were taken below to the cells to await their fate.

The jury returned thirty minutes later and all four were found guilty.

There still existed the conundrum of whether the four should be hanged for piracy. The foreman of the jury agreed the *Frederick* wasn't on the high seas and the men were not mariners, but the jury felt they needed to bring down a guilty verdict.

Justice Pedder would normally don the black cloth and sentence the men to death. They would have been hanged the next morning. In this case, though, he wanted to be sure that this truly was a legal case of piracy.

Pedder wrote a report to the Executive Council on May 8 1837, and he sought the council of Algernon Montagu, a Supreme Court judge and a former attorney general.

Pedder turned out to be the men's guardian angel and sentencing of the four was suspended indefinitely.

The *Hobart Town Courier* published a story two weeks after the trial.

THE
HOBART TOWN
COURIER.

Of what then have these men been guilty? That obeying the first impulse of human nature, they endeavoured to escape from slavery! That in the endeavour they not only not committed no enormity of any, the slightest, description – not even the breath of personal violence to any human being – but on the contrary, they exhibited so much forbearance in the manner in which they effected the purpose to which every feeling inherent in man so strongly induced them ...that the people they put on shore expressed themselves, according to their own evidence, in the warmest terms of gratitude! Is there, then, in any one act of their proceeding, any one feature deserving the last of punishments that man can inflict upon his fellow man – Death?

The four prisoners were still held in Hobart Gaol in chains with little opportunity for exercise.

James Porter began writing his memoirs.

William Elliston, a wealthy newspaper publisher, printed his first manuscript; it not only earned Porter some money but also made him famous.

July 1839

The four *Frederick* convicts were notified that their lives had been spared, but they were being transported to Norfolk Island for life. This island had an even more horrific history than Sarah Island.

The establishment was glad to get rid of these four criminals as they had been nothing but trouble. Not only were they chased halfway across the world and transported back, but they avoided hanging on a technicality.

Prime Ministers, governors and various other high officials heard pleas of their innocence. They had several newspaper articles written about them yet they were still just criminals.

Welcome to Norfolk Island

Chapter 16

The four men boarded the *Marion Watson*, heading for Sydney Town, on July 13 1839. The relatively short journey was similar to others they had experienced as guests of the Crown; they were down below and in chains.

Once they reached Sydney Town they were transferred to the *Governor Phillip*, arriving at Norfolk Island on August 28.

It seemed like an exile. They were on an island 1000 miles off the Australian coast; a rocky outcrop in the Pacific Ocean; an ocean they all knew well.

The prison commandant was Major Thomas Bunbury, a cruel and heartless tyrant. Bunbury would bring out the cat for the smallest of transgressions and enjoy witnessing the suffering.

Norfolk Island was New South Wales's version of Devil's Island and worse than Macquarie Harbour.

The *Frederick* four were very apprehensive when they arrived at what was meant to be their home for the remainder of their lives.

When Major Baylee took responsibility for Sarah Island the whole settlement changed for the better,

The same was true when Alexander Maconochie replaced the bastard Bunbury.

The *Frederick* four were fortunate the new commandant arrived soon after they did.

Maconochie was out to prove his theory that kindness and respect were more effective rehabilitators than flogging a man to within an inch of his life. He also was against solitary confinement and hanging was only the last resort.

The authorities, including Arthur, despised him and his methods, but he was in control.

The reason Maconochie was so different from his predecessors was that he had been a prisoner of the French during the Napoleonic wars. He had experienced harsh cruel treatment and promised himself that if he was ever in the position of commandant in a prison he would treat the prisoners well.

His first task was to order the gallows outside the barracks to be dismantled and taken away.

He banned the use of the double-knotted cat used by the floggers.

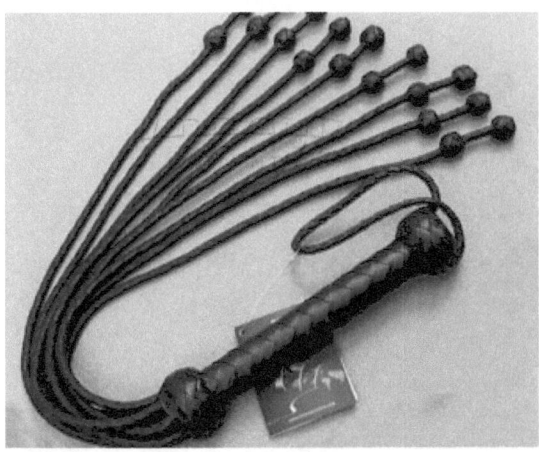

He believed the prisoners should have somewhere to pray so be built two churches: one Catholic and one Protestant. He demonstrated his egalitarian attitude by allocating a room in the barracks to house a synagogue.

Maconochie created a system of rewards and punishments that did not employ the whip. He introduced a marks based system so if a convict did something good he earned marks. If he did something bad marks were taken away. The convicts had an opportunity to reduce their sentence by accumulating points.

Maconochie created a library and encouraged the convicts to read authors such as Walter Scott and Robbie Burns. He purchased William Shakespeare's entire works. Many prisoners relished the opportunity to read such works.

Prisoners were also encouraged to write their own life stories, which were no doubt very interesting reading.

Porter wrote the second volume of his memoirs while on Norfolk Island.

1843

The *Frederick* four were released from captivity and returned to Sydney Town. James Porter had been transported to Australia in 1823 and twenty years later he was still up to his old tricks.

THE END

EPILOGUE

James Porter

Porter arrived back in Sydney Town in May 1843. In 1844 he moved to Newcastle where he was gaoled three times.

His crimes were minor; seven days for absenting and another seven for disobedience. His most serious crime was assault for which he was gaoled for fourteen days.

He redeemed himself by informing the police where an illegal still was located.

He expected to receive a reward for uncovering the still but received nothing.

He moved back to Sydney Town and was employed as a wardsman at Hyde Park Barracks.

In 1846 Porter was granted his ticket of leave, but less than a month later he was convicted for stealing and gaoled.

In May 1847 Porter escaped and was never heard of again. There was some conjecture that he returned to Chile.

Billy Shires

Billy returned to Sydney Town in 1843 and was transferred to Newcastle in 1845. He received his ticket of leave and was pardoned due to good conduct in 1849.

Charles Lyon

In October 1842 while in custody Lyon was caught 'conspiring to construct a boat'.

His punishment was two hundred lashes. He barely survived the flogging.

William Cheshire

Behaved himself after receiving his ticket of leave.

James Leslie

John Barker

John Fare

John Dady

Benjamin Russen

All escaped and lived in places unknown.

BIBLIOGRAPHY

CR   Convict Records: William Swallow

       London History · London, 1800-1913 · Central Criminal Court

BBC   BBC · GCSE Bitesize: Living conditions in cities

       Slums and Slumming in Late-Victorian London

W   Macquarie Harbour Penal Station · Wikipedia

W   Cyprus mutiny · Wikipedia

       1954_Pretyman_Pirates_at_Recherche_Bay.pdf

       William Swallow's Excellent Adventure | Mental Floss

       China Trade and the East India Company

VCP   At Sea · the Voyage and Conditions on Board · Victorian Crime and Punishment from E2BN

       Life on a Convict Ship · Western Australia

       Prison hulks on the River Thames · Crime and punishment · Port Cities

       A Day in the Life: Convicts on board Prison Hulks

       #claimaconvict: Convict details · William Swallow arrived 1831

       Convict Hulks | The Digital Panopticon

       Convict Ships to Australia

       Convict Ship Exmouth 1831

       14 Jul 1956 · CONVICT PIRATES MADE ONE SIMPLE MISTAKE SO... · Trove

W   Ching Shih · Wikipedia

       The Seizure of the "Cyprus" · Old Tales of a Young Country · Marcus Clarke, Book, etext

The Seizure of the "Cyprus" - Old Tales of a Young Country - Marcus Clarke, Book, etext

Tonga - Wikipedia   https://en.wikipedia.org/wiki/Tonga

The brig Cyprus: How an English surfer solved the mystery of an Australian pirate ship in Japan - ABC News (Australian Broadcasting Corporatio...

The Pirates of the Brig Cyprus: Frank Clune, P. R. Stephenson: Amazon.com: Books

The pirates of the brig Cyprus / Frank Clune and P.R. Stephensen. - Version details - Trove

11 Rules From an Actual Pirate Code | Mental Floss

Australian convict pirates in Japan: evidence of 1830 voyage unearthed | Australia news | The Guardian

Australian pirate tales - Australian National Maritime MuseumAustralian National Maritime Museum

Piracy on the Brig Cyprus

Cypress

Australian Folk Songs | Cyprus Brig

Ching Shih – from Prostitute to Pirate Lord | Ancient Origins

24 Feb 1831 - PIRATES OF THE CYPRUS. - Trove

Piracy Trial

The Newgate Calendar - WILLIAM SWALLOW, alias WALDON; GEORGE JAMES DAVIS, alias GEORGE HUNTLEY; WILLIAM WATTS, alias CHARLE...

The Great Escape: start reading The Ship That Never Was by Adam Courtenay – Better Reading

John Popjoy and the Mutiny on the Cyprus

Microsoft Word - Catalpa_draft.doc

Hiliday Ideas

James Porter and the capture of the Frederick · Hindsight - ABC Radio National (Australian Broadcasting Corporation)

Punishment

James Porter's 1838 narrative – Archives Office of Tasmania

Clarke M For the Term of His Natural Life

First published 2020 by Crabtree Pty Ltd

The Last Pirate Hanged is a work of fiction. Any resemblance to real persons, living or dead, is purely coincidental.

ISBN: 978-0-6484869-8-5 (pbk)
ISBN: 978-0-6484869-9-2 (ebk)